Willa couldn't remember ever feeling so isloated.

So alone. Not even in the middle of South Dakota, miles from the nearest town. Surely all the people looking for her would have a hard time finding her on Cape Diablo. But she didn't delude herself. She would never be safe. The sound of the boat motor died off into the distance. She looked back once but the boat had already disappeared from sight. All she could see was the horizon and the endless Gulf of Mexico.

As she looked up at the villa, she wondered if there was any place safe enough or far enough from civilization to elude the men who were on her trail.

If it wasn't Cape Diablo, then no place existed.

Willa stopped in front of the villa. She could hear the waves lapping at the dock and the wind whispering in the palms as if it were hiding some sinister secrets....

B.J. DANIELS

UNDENIABLE PROOF

TORONTO • NEW YORK • LONDON
AMSTERDAM • PARIS • SYDNEY • HAMBURG
STOCKHOLM • ATHENS • TOKYO • MILAN • MADRID
PRAGUE • WARSAW • BUDAPEST • AUCKLAND

This book is for Tim and Elise
who told us about these waters and gave us our first chart of the islands. Thank you for many hours boating through a blur of mangrove-green islands on endless water.
There is no neater place to be lost.

ISBN-13: 978-0-373-22936-9
ISBN-10: 0-373-22936-4

UNDENIABLE PROOF

This edition published by arrangement with Harlequin Books S.A.

www.eHarlequin.com

Printed in U.S.A.

ABOUT THE AUTHOR

B.J. Daniels's life dream was to write books. After a career as an award-winning newspaper journalist, she sold thirty-seven short stories before she finally wrote her first book. That book, *Odd Man Out*, received a 4½ star review from *Romantic Times BOOKclub* and went on to be nominated for Best Harlequin Intrigue of 1995. Since then she has won numerous awards, including a career achievement award for romantic suspense.

B.J. lives in Montana with her husband, Parker, two springer spaniels, Scout and Spot, and an aging, temperamental tomcat named Jeff. When she isn't writing, she snowboards, camps, boats and plays tennis. To contact B.J., write to her at P.O. Box 183, Bozeman, MT 59771, or check out her Web site at www.bjdaniels.com.

Books by B.J. Daniels

HARLEQUIN INTRIGUE

797—THE COWGIRL IN QUESTION†
803—COWBOY ACCOMPLICE†
845—AMBUSHED!†
851—HIGH-CALIBER COWBOY†
857—SHOTGUN SURRENDER†
876—WHEN TWILIGHT COMES
897—CRIME SCENE AT CARDWELL RANCH**
915—SECRET WEAPON SPOUSE
936—UNDENIABLE PROOF

†McCalls' Montana
**Montana Mystique

CAST OF CHARACTERS

Willa St. Clair—The artist's dreams were all coming true—until she witnessed a murder and was forced to hide on the island of Cape Diablo.

Landry Jones—His life depended on finding the artist and making sure she never testified against him.

Zeke Hartung—What had the undercover cop been thinking the night he died?

Freddy D.—He'd do anything to get the name of the man who'd betrayed him—and the missing evidence that could save him from prison.

Odell Grady—Was the writer working on a book about Cape Diablo? Or was he up to something that could get him killed?

Henrietta "Henri" LaFrance—The good-looking redhead had come to the island to escape a bad relationship. Or had she?

Blossom—All Cape Diablo needed was a surly teenaged actress.

Alma Garcia—The former nanny had been on Cape Diablo so long everyone thought she was crazy.

Carlos Lazario—The old fisherman moved around the island like a ghost.

Chapter One

He'd waited too long. They knew. The realization turned his blood to ice water. If they knew that he had the disk, then they also knew what he planned to do with it.

He felt the full weight of the disk in his breast pocket. In the right hands, the disk was gold. In the wrong hands, it was a death warrant.

Simon didn't look back but he knew they were behind him, following him. Two of them. He could hear them. Feel them working their way along the dark street.

All he could guess is that they weren't sure where he was headed. They would want to know who he'd planned to give the disk to. He had a pretty good idea that they knew exactly who he worked for—but just wanted proof.

He'd changed course the moment he'd heard them behind and now found himself headed for the beach. Ahead was the artsy part of St. Pete Beach, the small southern Florida town at the edge of the Gulf of Mexico.

Art galleries, studios, little shops. All closed this time of the night.

No place to hide.

He had to ditch the disk. It was his only chance. He was probably a dead man either way, but he might be able to talk his way out of this if the disk wasn't found on him.

Ahead Simon spotted a light burning in one of the art studios. Was it possible it was still open? Could he be that lucky?

He could hear the quickening of the men's steps behind him as he neared the shop entrance. Inside, the light silhouetted a figure at the back of the shop apparently working late. His good luck. That person's bad fortune.

It took everything in him not to run. But that would make him look guilty. That would get him killed before he could hide the disk.

Simon reached the front door of the shop and grasped the knob. He could see a woman working in the studio at the back. The men behind him were so close he thought he could feel their collective breaths on his neck. As he tried the door, he expected to feel a hand drop to his shoulder and a cold steel barrel press against his backbone.

Locked! He couldn't catch his breath. He jiggled the doorknob. His heart pounded so hard, all he could hear was the blood buzzing in his ears.

The woman who'd been working at the back looked up. Obviously she hadn't been expecting anyone.

Simon waved and called to her in a voice he didn't recognize as his own, "Sorry I'm late."

Surprise registered in her eyes, but she stopped what she was doing and walked toward the door.

He thought he heard the two men slide back into the darker shadows as the woman opened the door.

"I'm sorry I'm so late," he said, stepping in, forcing her to step aside as he pushed past and into the shop. "I was afraid you'd already gone home. I called about one of your—" he glanced to see what kind of work the woman did "—paintings," he said, and stuffed his hands into his pockets so she didn't see how badly they were shaking as he turned to look at her.

He'd thought her twenty-something but she could have been younger. It was hard to tell her age with such pale skin sprinkled with golden freckles and blond hair that she had pulled back in a single long braid that trailed down her back. She wore a sleeveless T-shirt, peach-colored, and a pair of denim cropped pants. He caught the scent of vanilla.

"I'm sorry," she said, looking confused. "Are you sure you have the right gallery?" Simon could see that she was scared. If she only knew. But she closed the door behind her, failing, he noted, to lock it, though. Would the two men come in here after him? He couldn't be sure.

But if they did, the woman was as good as dead.

"Yes, this is the shop," he said, improvising as he moved to look at one of the Florida landscapes done in pastels. "My wife said she was told someone would be here late." A man with a wife would make her feel safer, he hoped, as he saw that she hadn't moved. In fact, she seemed to hover by the phone on the desk by the door.

He thought of the real wife he'd had. She'd left him because she couldn't take the line of work he was in. Low pay, ridiculous hours and always the chance that tonight might be the night he didn't come home. Tonight might be the night she got the phone call. Or worse, opened the door in the wee hours of the morning to see one of his buddies at the door bearing the bad news.

He studied one of the signed paintings, trying to focus. Thinking about Evie right now was a really bad idea. Next to it was a poster announcing an art show at a gallery down the street tomorrow night. "Are you W. St. Clair?"

"Yes." She sounded shy, maybe a little embarrassed. Or maybe it was just nerves with him in her studio this late at night. He could see where she'd been framing some paintings at a workbench in the back.

"You say someone told your wife I would be here late?" she asked. He could hear her trying to come up with an explanation. "I can't imagine who would have told her that."

He shrugged and moved through the paintings, trying not to look out the front windows. Just act normal. The thought almost made him laugh. A normal man would be smart enough not to have gotten caught. And he was caught. Even if he ditched the disk, he wasn't sure he could save himself. Those men wouldn't be after him unless they knew he'd double-crossed them.

"I had to work late myself tonight," Simon said, making it up as he went. Nothing new there. "I was afraid I wouldn't get here in time. You see it's our anniversary. Ten years. My wife told me about a painting she saw here and I thought it would make a great anniversary present for her."

Evie had bailed after six years. Hadn't even waited for the seven-year itch.

"Your anniversary?" The artist smiled. She wanted to believe him. Simon knew he was laying it on a little thick but he needed her to feel safe. To act as if she'd known he was coming. Act as if nothing was wrong for the men who he knew were outside watching him. Watching them both.

The ploy seemed to be working. He saw her relax a little, her movements not as tense as she stepped away from the front windows.

"Do you mind if I just look around for a few minutes?" he asked. "I know I'll recognize the painting she fell in love with from the way she described it."

"If you tell me—"

"You do beautiful work. I can understand why she was so taken with your paintings," he said, cutting her off.

"Thank you," she said, sounding less suspicious although clearly still cautious. "I have a show coming up tomorrow night so I was working late framing. I'm afraid some of the paintings aren't for sale—at least until the show tomorrow night. I hope your wife didn't choose one that's tagged for the show."

"Well, if she did, I'm sure I'll find something that she'll love." Simon heard her go back to the bench. All she had to do was look up and see him from where she worked. He continued to move through the paintings, pretending to admire each as if in no hurry to find the one his wife wanted.

There was only one spot in the small shop where she wouldn't be able to see him. Nor would anyone outside have a clear view because of several large paintings that hung from a makeshift wall.

He found a painting that was marked For Show, Not For Sale and slipped the knife from his pocket. He quickly cut a small slot along the edge of the paper backing the framed painting—one of a colorful sailboat keeling over in the wind—and slid the disk inside between the paper and the artwork.

The disk fit snug enough that it made no sound when Simon picked up the painting as if inspecting it more closely. No one should notice the careful cut he'd made. Not that anyone would get the chance. He'd be back tonight for the painting just as soon as he got rid of the two men after him.

He breathed a sigh of relief as he picked up another small painting of a Florida street market, colorful and quaint and the painting was not tagged for the show.

"This is the one. What does the W. stand for?" he asked as he took it over to her.

"Willa." She smiled as she saw which painting he had selected. "An excellent choice."

Simon paid in cash and watched her carefully wrap it, priding himself on the fact that he hadn't once glanced toward the front windows. Anyone watching him from outside would think this had been his destination all along. At least he hoped so. Everything was riding on this.

"You really saved my life," he said, smiling at the young woman. "I can't tell you how relieved I was to see that you were still around tonight."

She handed him the package and smiled back. "Happy anniversary. I hope your wife enjoys the painting."

"Oh, she will." Evie would have had a fit if he'd brought home a painting by an unknown. Evie liked nice things. And Simon had failed to give her what she needed.

Swallowing down the bitterness, he idly picked up one of the flyers by the cash register announcing Willa St. Clair's gallery showing the next evening and pretended to study it before he folded the flyer and put it into the breast pocket of his jacket.

She followed him to the door.

"Good luck with your show tomorrow night," he said as she started to close the door. "Maybe my wife and I will stop by."

"It's just down the street, at the Seaside Seascapes Gallery."

Simon nodded as she closed and locked it behind him, then he turned and started back the way he'd come, taking his time, the small painting tucked under his arm.

He waited for the two men to accost him as he walked down the street. Two blocks from Willa St. Clair's art studio, and he hadn't seen anyone who wanted to kill him. Maybe he'd been wrong. Maybe he'd hidden the disk and blown off his delivery meeting for nothing.

He should have been relieved. But instead, it made him angry. He'd panicked for nothing. Now he would have to go back and get the damned disk after the studio was closed. Worse, he would have to set up another delivery meeting. Any change of plans always increased the danger.

At his car, he beeped open the doors, the lights flashed and he reached for the door handle.

They came at him from out of the darkness, surprising him. Simon reached for his weapon, but he wasn't fast enough. The small painting he'd bought fell to the ground with a thud as the larger of the two grabbed him, the smaller one taking his gun and searching him.

"What the hell do *you* want?" he bluffed, recognizing them both. "You scared the hell out of me. You're damned lucky I didn't shoot you both."

The smaller of the two men scooped up the painting from the sidewalk and tore the canvas from its frame, tossing it aside when he didn't find what he was looking for.

Simon considered whether he could take them both and decided he'd be dead before he even had one of them down. No, he thought, he had a much better chance if he could get them to take him to their boss. He'd managed to bluff his way this far. He had to believe he could get himself out of this, as well.

"Where is it?" the small one demanded as he jammed a gun into Simon's kidneys.

He groaned. "Where's what?" The big one hit him before Simon even saw him move. The punch dropped him to his knees.

"Not here," the smaller one snapped and Simon heard the sound of a car engine.

A moment later he was shoved onto the floorboard of the back seat, something heavy pressed on top of him.

He tried to breathe, to remain calm. The disk was hidden. If he played his cards right, he could get it back and still make delivery. Too much was at stake to give up now.

If there was one thing Simon Renton was good at it, it was talking his way out of trouble. Didn't everyone say he was like a cat with nine lives?

He just hoped he hadn't run out of lives.

Chapter Two

Simon was dead.

Landry Jones stood in the large office of the Tampa warehouse fighting the urge to put a bullet hole into the brains of the two men who'd killed Simon. Stupid fools.

But then he'd have to take out their boss, Freddy D., and that wasn't part of the plan. At least not yet.

"We almost got him to tell us who he was working with," said the larger of the two thugs, who went by TNT or T for short, no doubt because of the man's short fuse.

The other man, known as Worm, was smaller, cagier and meaner if that were possible. "I told T to back off a little but Simon was giving him a lot of grief."

Knowing Simon, he would have purposely got T going, so the fool killed him before he gave up the names of the other undercover cops who'd infiltrated the organization.

Landry swore under his breath. "That's why I wanted to handle this. I would have gotten the names out of him."

Freddy D. studied him from beneath hooded gray eyes. "Maybe. Maybe not."

Landry shook his head angrily. "So where's the disk Simon supposedly made?" he asked the two thugs. "Or did you kill him before he told you that, as well?"

"Easy," Freddy D. said, but turned his big bald head to take in T and Worm. "Tell me you got the disk." The tone of his voice made it pretty clear that T and Worm might not be around long if they didn't.

Landry held his breath. T squirmed but Worm looked almost cocky. "He told us where to find it," Worm said.

Landry let out the breath he'd been holding. "Great. You don't have the disk, you don't even know if it exists or if Simon *was* a cop or not." He felt the corpse-gray eyes of Freddy D. shift to him again.

"My source said he *was* a cop and that there were two others working with him in my organization," Freddy D. said.

"Yeah? And what if your source just wanted Simon dead and you running scared of your own men?" Landry asked, knowing he was stepping over the line. "Simon was smart. He was good for business. Now he's dead and there might not even be a damned disk."

"Cool down..." Zeke said from where he lounged against the wall. Zeke Hartung, known affectionately as Zeke the Freak, was tall and slim with rebel good looks. Landry had never asked how he got the nickname. He didn't want to know.

"We all liked Simon," Zeke continued. "If he was a cop, then I'm a cop and I'm taking you all in."

The men in the room laughed nervously. Landry met Zeke's gaze. Zeke smiled. The bastard loved to bluff.

"If your source says there's a disk, Freddy D., then there's a disk," Zeke continued. "So let's find it. Find out what's on it. Find out where Simon got his information—or if these two morons killed the wrong man."

"Who you calling a moron?" T demanded, going for Zeke.

Freddy D. stopped it with a wave of his hand. "Zeke's right. Once we have the disk, then we'll know who we can trust. So where is this disk and why don't I have it yet?" Freddy D. asked, a knife edge to his voice.

Even Worm looked a little less sure of himself. "Simon said he hid it in a painting in one of those art studios down by the beach."

"You think he's a cop, you think he has information on a disk that will bring down the entire organization or make it possible for some other organization to move in on us, and you trusted him to tell you the truth about where he hid it?" Landry demanded incredulously.

Freddy D. shot Landry a look that dropped his blood temperature to just above freezing before turning that cold stare on T and Worm. "So why didn't you just get the painting and bring it to me?"

Worm swallowed, his Adam apple bobbing up and down. "It's in this art studio. The thing is the shops are all open now. We can't just waltz in and take the painting in broad daylight."

Freddy D. sat up, his weight making the chair groan. "Don't *take* it, you fool. *Buy* it. How much money do you need?"

T and Worm exchanged a look. "It's not for sale."

Freddy D. sat back as if Worm had slapped him. "You aren't serious."

"The painting is part of an art show tonight at some gallery called Seaside Seascapes," Worm said. "I just thought I'd go to the show tonight and buy the painting."

Freddy D. groaned. "You? At an art show?"

"Better than sending T," Landry said.

Freddy D. swiveled around in his chair to pin Landry with that corpse-gray gaze again. "You go, Jones. T and Worm will be waiting for you in the alley to make sure there are no problems. You buy the painting, make sure you get it tonight, you hand it over. They'll be watching you the whole time. Have a problem with that?"

"That's assuming T and Worm aren't undercover cops," Landry said sarcastically.

Even Freddy D. laughed at that.

"I don't know. They're dumb enough to be cops," Zeke said.

Both men looked like they could kill Zeke, but were smart enough not to try. At least not right now in front of the boss.

"I don't want those two in the alley," Landry said. He knew the best thing he could do right now was to go along with Freddy D.'s plan. But it was too late in Landry's life to do the best thing. Far from it.

"Think about it, these two hanging out in the alley behind a fancy art gallery?" Landry said. "First off, anyone who sees them is going to call the cops, thinking they're staking out the place. Secondly, if your source is right and Simon was a cop working with the feds and had made a disk he planned to hand over, then the feds are looking for this disk, too."

Freddy D. narrowed his eyes at him, and for a moment Landry thought he might tell T and Worm to kill him. "While not eloquent or wise, you do make a good point. You're saying that Simon might have gotten the feds word where he hid the disk."

Landry doubted it. Otherwise the feds would be busting down the doors right now, guns blazing. "I think it would be a mistake to underestimate Simon. I know if I was him and I spotted these two behind me, guilty or not, I'd do whatever I could to cover my ass."

"I'll cover the alley," Zeke said. "Or better yet, I'll go to the art show and let Landry wait in the sidelines."

"Like you know squat about art," Landry said, then pretended not to care. "Whatever."

Freddy D. raised a hand. "Landry goes in. Zeke, you take the alley. T and Worm won't be far away just in case."

Just in case any of them thought about double-crossing him. "I want that disk," the boss said.

"If it exists," Landry added, and Freddy D. gave him a warning look before turning again to T and Worm.

"What do we know about this artist where Simon said he hid the disk?"

The thugs exchanged confused looks.

"The painting he had on him was signed W. St. Clair," Worm said. "Simon said her name was Willow."

"Or something like that," T said. "He wasn't talking too clearly."

Freddy D. groaned. "What about the artist? Is it possible she's his contact?"

"You hear sirens?" Zeke asked sarcastically. "If the feds had the disk we'd all be facedown and handcuffed."

"Zeke's right," Landry said. "So what does this painting look like? You did get that, right?"

Worm looked like he was itching to punch Landry's ticket. "It's a painting of a sailboat. It had a red and white sail and the boat was blue. The boat is at full sail and there is a blond woman at the wheel. Her hair's blowing back and she's kind of hanging off to the side like she's having a great time."

Landry stared at Worm, amazed they'd gotten that much information out of Simon about the painting but weren't sure about the artist's name. He wanted to believe that Simon had made up every word of it. But Landry had seen T in action and knew that few men could withstand that form of torture. Even Simon.

"I'll find the painting," Landry said.

"I also think it would be wise to find out what the woman knows about Simon," Freddy D. said. "Either way, she's a loose end." Freddy D. was looking straight at him. "You have a way with the ladies, Landry. Take care of her."

WILLA ST. CLAIR GLANCED around the gallery at all her paintings hanging on the walls and could no longer suppress her excitement. She still couldn't believe it. All the hard work, the long hours painting then framing, had finally paid off.

Just when she thought that her life couldn't get any better than this, she saw the handsome dark-haired man standing by the door.

He'd caught her eye several times earlier, lifting his wineglass and giving her a nod. She'd felt herself warm, complimented by his attention.

Now he smiled and she saw that the crowd had thinned. Clearly he was waiting for her. Her heart beat a little faster.

Several of the stragglers came over to congratulate her. Like her first two openings, this one had been an incredible success. She still couldn't believe it. Almost all of the paintings had small red dots on them, indicating they were sold.

Her dream had come true. She tried to calm her runaway heart, took a deep breath and turned to look toward the door.

He was gone.

Her disappointment pierced the helium high she'd

been riding on just moments before. She'd taken too long. He'd gotten tired of waiting.

She couldn't help feeling regret. He'd made a point of getting her attention during the show. But each time she hadn't been able to get away to talk to him. She'd hoped he would find a way to talk to her before the evening was over.

"Great show, sweetie," the gallery owner, Evan Charles, said, coming over to give her an air kiss beside each cheek. "Everyone was just raving about your use of color. You're a hit."

She thanked Evan and promised to let him know when she had enough paintings ready for another show. Taking her wrap from the closet by the door, she stepped out into the Florida night air, closed her eyes and breathed it all in as he locked up behind her.

You're not in South Dakota anymore.

She smiled to herself. She would never tire of breathing sea air. She could hear the cry of the gulls and the lull of the surf not a block away. She loved Florida. And Florida, it seemed, loved her.

"Beautiful night," said a male voice as warm and silky as the night air. "Beautiful woman."

She opened her eyes and turned already smiling, knowing it was him. He *had* waited for her.

"Congratulations," he said. "I was hoping all evening to get a chance to meet you. You were much too popular. And I was much too shy." He grinned and extended his hand. "Landry Jones."

He was anything but shy, she thought as her hand disappeared into his large one. His touch was gentle but there was raw power behind it. She shivered as she looked into his dark eyes, and he grinned as if he knew exactly what she was thinking.

Amazingly, he was even more striking up close. Not classically handsome. Too rough around the edges for that. He wore khaki chinos and a palm-tree-print short-sleeved shirt and deck shoes. He was tanned and the fingers on his left hand were scraped as if he'd been in a fistfight. He looked like a man who could hold his own in a fight, she thought, as a niggling worry wormed its way into her perfect night.

Landry Jones wasn't the type of man a woman met at an art showing. Especially not hers.

"So, you're interested in Florida landscapes?" she asked, cocking her head to one side. "You don't seem the type."

He feigned hurt, laughed and gave her a sheepish grin. "Actually I'm more interested in the artist, although I find both intriguing."

She felt her cheeks heat under his compliment as well as his dark piercing gaze. If he was trying to charm her, he was doing a darned good job. "Thank you." She wanted to pinch herself. This night was just too good to be true.

"Any chance I could buy you a cup of coffee?" he asked. "Now that we've officially met? There's a coffee shop I know that's still open not far from here. Or if you'd like something stronger..."

If only this night never had to end. And Landry Jones was like the topping on the cake. And maybe the ice cream, as well.

So what if he wasn't the type to frequent art shows? For tonight he could be her type, she thought with a thrill.

"Coffee would be great." She couldn't trust herself with anything stronger, not while feeling as exhilarated as she was already.

"Coffee it is then," he said, his smile mesmerizing. "This night calls for a celebration. If you're feeling adventurous, we could even have a piece of key lime pie."

She was feeling adventurous, all right.

"My car is just over here." He pointed down the dark street and suddenly she wasn't so sure.

She knew she was being silly. But suddenly the reality of the situation hit her. This wasn't South Dakota and she didn't know this man from Adam.

The idea of getting into a car with a complete stranger was totally alien to her—and suddenly seemed more than a little dangerous.

Odd as it might seem, she knew everyone back in her small hometown in South Dakota and never dated anyone she didn't. Now she was about to get into a car with a stranger she'd met just moments before.

While she could hear traffic a few streets over, there was no longer anyone around, all the shops and galleries were now closed and she was feeling a little vulnerable.

She turned, hoping Evan was still inside closing up.

Even the gallery lights were out. She hadn't seen Evan leave, but then all her attention had been on Landry Jones, hadn't it?

Landry must have seen her indecision and the way her feet were rooted to the sidewalk. "Wait here. I'll get the car." He flashed a reassuring smile, then turned and keyed his remote. A set of headlights flashed down the street. She watched him walk toward a newer-model blue BMW, telling herself she was being very foolish.

Yes, she was taking a chance, but hadn't she had to take a chance when she'd left South Dakota to come to Florida? And look how that had worked out. Sometimes you had to take a chance.

Especially with a handsome man on one of the most exciting nights of her life.

She groaned as she took a few steps down the street away from the gallery—and Landry Jones. With her luck, the man would turn out to be a serial killer ax murderer. Otherwise, it was almost as if he was too perfect.

AT THE CAR, Landry climbed in and pulled out his cell. He punched speed dial as he watched Willa St. Clair.

"The painting wasn't in the show," he said the moment the line was answered. He could see Willa St. Clair waiting for him. "But don't worry. I'll find it. I have the artist in my crosshairs right now, so to speak. Tell Zeke I won't be needing him. I'll call when I have the disk." He snapped his cell shut before Freddy D. could argue.

With a start, he saw that Willa St. Clair was walking down the block toward the alley behind the gallery.

He swore as he noticed the change in her. She'd looked a little leery earlier when he'd asked her out. But now she appeared scared and, unless he missed his guess, about to change her mind.

She hadn't been what he'd expected. One look at her and he'd known he'd have to handle her with kid gloves. At least until he got her in the car.

Now he had to move fast. Once he had her under his control, he told himself, it would be smooth sailing. He grimaced at his own inside joke.

Where the hell was this sailboat painting that Simon had told T and Worm he'd hid the disk in? Landry had come to believe it existed. Simon was smart enough to know that by telling T and Worm, he would also be telling the rest of them. That could explain the intricate description Simon had given the two goons.

But as Landry's luck would have it, the painting T and Worm described wasn't in the gallery show.

So where was it?

T. and Worm had said that some blond woman had been working at the back of the art studio last night when Simon had gone in. Their description of her matched the artist's—Willa St. Clair.

She was the key to finding the painting—and ultimately the disk. And Willa St. Clair was going to tell him. One way or another, Landry would have that disk before the night was over.

As he reached to start the car engine and go after her, he heard a soft tap on his side window. He turned and glanced up, only half surprised to see Zeke standing next to his car.

"What the hell do you want?" he asked as he powered down his side window. "Didn't Freddy D. tell you to call it a night?"

Zeke smiled. "Change of plans, old buddy."

WILLA KNEW she would hate herself in the morning if she didn't go out with Landry Jones. For the rest of her life, she would think of him, actually building him up in her memory—if that were possible—and always wonder what might have been.

She stopped walking up the block and turned, blinking as she looked back. The BMW hadn't moved but she could hear the purr of the engine. As her eyes adjusted to the darkness she saw that a man was standing beside the driver's side talking to Landry.

Now was her chance to just disappear. Take the coward's way out. Run!

Funny, but that's exactly what her instincts told her to do.

Pop! Pop! The sound took her by surprise. She stared, unable to move even when she saw the glint of a gun through the windshield, saw the flash as Landry Jones fired two more shots.

The man next to the car staggered back, slammed

into the wall and slid slowly down, his head dropping to his chest.

Poleaxed, she stared at the dead man—her first dead man—her mind screaming: Landry shot him! He *shot* him!

She felt Landry shift his gaze to her and suddenly she was moving, kicking off her high heels and running for her life. She could hear the roar of the BMW engine as he came after her, the headlights washing over her.

A main street was only two blocks away. She could see the lights of the traffic. There would be people around. She could get away, get help. But she knew she would never reach it. The BMW was bearing down on her.

She glanced back and blinded by the headlights didn't see the man with two dogs on leashes appear out of the darkness off to her right.

The man avoided crashing into her, but she got caught up in the dogs' leashes and went down hard.

"Are you all right? I'm sorry I didn't see you," the man said, sounding distraught as he knelt beside her.

"Help me," she cried, not yet feeling the pain. "He's going to kill me."

"Who?" the man asked, glancing around.

She managed to sit up, vaguely aware that her hands and knees were scraped raw from hitting the sidewalk. The street was dark. No BMW. No Landry Jones.

Three sets of eyes stared at her at ground level, only one set human. The dogs were big and wonderfully muttlike. The man knelt next to her, looking scared and upset.

Willa began to cry. "That car that was chasing me…."

"It went on past," the man said.

Her hands and knees began to ache and she saw that her dress that she'd bought especially for the showing was ruined. Her new shoes were back down the street where she'd kicked them off.

"Are you sure the car was chasing you?"

One of the dogs licked her in the face. She put her arm around its neck, hugging it tightly for a moment before she dug her cell phone out of her purse and punched in 911.

Chapter Three

Landry couldn't believe how badly things had gone. What a nightmare. Simon was dead. So was Zeke. Zeke.

He put his head in his hands. What the hell had happened?

Unfortunately, he knew the answer to that, he thought as he gingerly touched his side. He'd been lucky. Although the wound had bled like hell, it hadn't been life threatening. Still, he'd had a hell of a time finding a doctor to stitch him up and make sure it didn't get infected. It wasn't like he could just walk into an emergency room. By law, doctors were required to report gunshot wounds.

He'd had to find a doctor he could trust not to turn him in. He couldn't chance using Freddy D.'s or any of the ones the cops knew about.

The wound, though, had turned out to be the least of his problems. Since that night, he'd been a hunted man. Willa St. Clair's eyewitness testimony that he'd shot

Zeke Hartung down in cold blood had every cop on the force and the feds after him—not to mention Freddy D. and his boys.

For days Landry had been on the run, keeping his head down, but he'd known from the get-go that he couldn't keep this up. He had to find that damned disk. The proof he needed was on it. Without the disk, he was a dead man.

He'd come close to getting the girl—and in the long run, the disk. He still had a few friends on the force he could trust, ones that wouldn't believe he was a dirty cop, even if he was, and one of them had given him the safe house location where Willa St. Clair was being held.

Unfortunately, Freddy D.'s men must have had an inside source as well because they hit the house before Landry could.

He'd almost had Willa St. Clair, though. He'd been so damned close he'd smelled the citrus scent of her shampoo in her long blond hair. But she'd managed to get away from not only him, but also Freddy D.'s men. The woman had either known about the hit on the safe house or she was damned lucky.

Like the night of her art show. If that fool with the two dogs hadn't come out of nowhere, Landry would have caught up to her, got her into the car and he'd have the disk by now and be calling the shots instead of running for his life.

But she'd seen him kill Zeke and he had known getting her into the car that night would have been near impossible if she'd been alone. Landry was good but he couldn't have taken on the guy with the two big dogs, too. And Freddy D. had said T and Worm would be nearby. If they'd seen him kill Zeke, then he couldn't be sure what those two fools would do.

He would be sitting behind bars right now or dead if he hadn't gotten the hell out of there.

So he'd disappeared into one of the small old-fashioned motels along the beach, blending in as best he could with the tourists, waiting for his cell phone to ring with news.

Since the safe house hit, he'd been hot on the trail of Willa St. Clair. His one fear was that someone would get to her before he did. There was no way she would last long out there on her own. That's why he had to get to her first. It was now a matter of life and death. His.

His cell rang. He took a breath, hoping that one of his cop friends he could trust had come through for him. But Zeke had friends too, friends who were taking his death personally and would shoot first and ask questions later if they found Landry.

"Hey," he said into the phone.

"This may be nothing…but I ran her cell phone. Willa St. Clair made a couple of calls. You want the numbers?"

Landry closed his eyes and let out the breath he'd been holding. "Oh, yeah. I owe you big-time."

"Yeah, you do." His friend read off the numbers. One in Naples. The other in South Dakota.

He hung up and tried the Naples one first. An answering machine picked up. She'd called a law firm? He almost hung up but heard something in the recording that caught his attention.

"...if you've called about the apartments on Cape Diablo island..."

Cape Diablo? Where the hell was that?

Five minutes later, a Florida map spread across the table in his motel, Landry Jones found Cape Diablo in an area known as Ten Thousand Islands at the end of the road on the Gulf Coast side almost to the tip of Florida.

The only other call Willa St. Clair made had been to South Dakota to probably friends or parents. So he was betting she'd rented one of the apartments on Cape Diablo.

Landry couldn't believe his luck. The woman was a novice at this. Plus she had no idea about the type of people after her. Or the resources they had at their disposal. She thought she'd found herself the perfect place to hide, did she? Instead, she'd just boxed herself in with no way out.

WILLA PULLED the baseball cap down on her now short curly auburn hair and squinted out across the rough water. The wind blew the tops off the waves in a spray of white mist. Past the bay she could see nothing but a line of green along the horizon.

She glanced at the small fishing boat and the man waiting for her to step in. He called himself Gator, wore flip-flops, colorful Bermuda shorts and a well-worn blue short-sleeved vented fishing shirt. His skin was dark from what he professed had been most of his fifty-some years in the south Florida sun.

"You want to go to the island or not?" he asked, seeming amused by her uncertainty.

"Maybe we should wait until it's not so rough out there," she suggested.

He laughed and shook his head. "We wait, the tide will go out and there is no going anywhere until she comes back in. You want to wait until the middle of the night?"

She didn't, and this time when he held out his hand she passed him the two suitcases and large cardboard box, containing what was most precious to her.

He set everything in the bottom of the boat and reached for her hand. She gave it to him and stepped in. The boat rocked wildly, forcing her to sit down hard on the wooden seat at the front of the boat. "I haven't been in a lot of boats."

"No kiddin'," he said, and started the outboard, flipping it around so the boat nosed backward into the waves.

She grabbed the metal sides and hung on.

"Might want to put on that jacket," he said as he tucked a tarp around her large cardboard box. "It could get a little wet."

A slight understatement. A wave slammed over the bow half drowning her in cold spray. She heard a chuckle behind her as she let go to hurriedly pull on the crumpled rain jacket he'd indicated, then drew a life preserver on over that. Both smelled of dead fish, and not for the first time, she wondered if this wasn't a mistake.

The boat swung around and cut bow first through the waves. Gator gave the motor more power. She gripped the seat under her as the boat rose and fell, jarring her each time it came down. She was glad she hadn't taken Gator's advice and eaten something first.

As they started across the bay, she turned to glance back at Chokoloskee, afraid she hadn't been as careful as she should have.

The wind snapped a flag hanging from the mast of a small sailboat back at the dock. The half-dozen stone crab fishermen she'd seen mending a large net on the dirt near one of the fish shacks were still hard at work. Several of the men had been curious when she'd walked down the dock to talk to Gator, but soon lost interest.

There was no one else on the docks. No new cars parked along the street where she'd hired Gator to take her out to the island. She tried to assure herself that there was no way she'd been followed. But it was hard, given what had happened while she'd been in protective custody.

Landry had found her in what was supposed to be a safe house with two armed policemen guarding her. She'd been lucky to get out alive. From the shots she'd heard behind her, the two men guarding her hadn't been as lucky. She didn't kid herself. Landry was after her.

Especially now that she was on her own, unarmed and running for her life. Nor did she doubt that the next time he found her, he'd try to finish what he'd started back at the safe house.

That's why she couldn't let him find her. Even if it meant doing something that she now considered just as dangerous.

The green on the horizon grew closer and she saw that it wasn't one large island but dozens of small ones, all covered in mangrove forests.

Gator steered the boat into what looked more like a narrow ditch, just wide enough for the small fishing boat. As he winded his way through one waterway after another past one island after another, she tried to memorize the route in case she needed to ever take a boat and get to the mainland on her own.

It was impossible. When she looked back, the islands melded together into nothing but what appeared to be an unbroken line of green. She couldn't even see where the water cut between the islands anymore.

Tamping down her growing panic that she'd jumped from the frying pan into the fire, she told herself she'd picked this island because it was hard to find. She'd wanted remote, and what was more remote than an island in the area known as Ten Thousand Islands along the Gulf side of the southern tip of Florida?

She'd heard about Cape Diablo through another artist she'd met. The woman, a graphic designer named Carrie Bishop, had rented an apartment in an old Spanish villa on the remote island. That's the last she saw of the artist but she remembered the woman telling her that the area had always been a haven for smugglers, drug runners and anyone who wanted to disappear and never be found.

That would be Willa St. Clair she thought, as watched the horizon, anxious to see what she'd gotten herself into. The rent had been supercheap. The apartment was described as furnished but basic. Not that beggars could be choosers. She was desperate, and that had meant taking desperate measures.

The sun dipped into the Gulf, turning the water's surface gold and silhouetting the islands ahead and behind her. Willa wondered how much farther it was to Cape Diablo and was about to ask when she felt the boat slow.

She looked up and caught a glimpse of red tile roof. A moment later the house came into view. Instantly she wanted to paint it. A haunting Spanish villa set among the palms.

With relief she saw a pier and beyond it an old two-story boathouse, thankful she would soon be off the rough water and on solid ground again.

Gator eased the boat, stepping out to tie off before he offered her a hand.

The boat wobbled wildly as she climbed out on the pier, making Gator chuckle again. She shot him a warning look, then turned her gaze to the villa.

It was truly breathtaking. Or at least it had been before it had fallen into disrepair. The Spanish-style structure now seemed to be battling back the vegetation growing up around it. Vines grew out of cracks or holes in the walls. Others climbed up the sides, hiding entire sections of the structure.

Palm trees swayed in the breeze and through an archway she could see what appeared to be a courtyard and possibly a swimming pool.

This had been the right decision, she thought, staring at the villa. It gave her the strangest feeling. Almost as if she was supposed to have come here. As if she had been born to paint it. Silly, but she felt as if the house had a story it needed told. That there was much more here than just crumbling walls.

Movement caught her eye. She looked upward and glimpsed someone watching her from a third-floor window.

"You change your mind?" Gator asked from behind her.

She turned to see that he'd put her suitcases on the dock and was sitting in his boat, obviously anxious to leave. Apparently this was as far as he went with her suitcases and box. So much for chivalry.

She turned to look at the villa again. "It's incredible, isn't it?"

He grunted.

She'd rented the apartment sight unseen through a phone number she'd called. Her rent had been paid via mail. So she wasn't surprised there was no one to meet her. She'd been told that the caretaker lived in the boathouse near the pier but that he might not be around. If there was an emergency or any problems, he was the man to see. Her rent money would be picked up each month when a supply boat came. She was told to talk to a man named Bull to order what she needed since there was no phone on the island. No electricity other than a generator. And cell phones didn't work from the island.

She'd wanted to disappear to someplace isolated—well, she had.

"Last chance," Gator said.

She shook her head.

He shrugged and glanced toward the Gulf of Mexico where the sun had sunk into the sea. "Then I'll shove off." He looked past her toward the house and seemed hesitant to leave her here—just as he'd been to bring her to the island in the first place. He'd tried to talk her out of it, asking if she knew anything about Cape Diablo.

"Why would you want to go out there?" he'd asked, pinning her with narrowed brown eyes. "Only people who are running from something or searching for it go out there. Few find what they're looking for. Usually just the opposite. Most wish they hadn't looked. Why do you think it is called Cape Diablo?"

"What are you telling me? That the island is haunted?" Her graphic artist friend had told her the island had an interesting history but hadn't elaborated.

"More like cursed."

Willa had anxiously looked over her shoulder, half expecting to see Landry.

"Running from something, huh?"

"Not that it's any of your business, but I'm trying to

get away from my ex-boyfriend, if you must know." She'd touched the bruise on her cheek that she'd gotten when the safe house the cops had put her in had been attacked.

Gator had given her a slow knowing nod, reached for the cash she'd offered him and hadn't tried to talk her out of it.

But clearly he hadn't wanted to bring her out here. Nor did he seem to want to leave her here. She thought about asking him why as he paused, then started the outboard.

"Send word by a fisherman or anyone heading to the mainland and I'll come get you," he said, his gaze softening. "Even if it's in the middle of the night."

Why would she want to leave in the middle of the night? His look said it wouldn't be long before she couldn't wait to get out off the island.

He touched the brim of his cap and turned the bow back the way they'd come. At least she thought it was the way they'd come.

She picked up the suitcases from the pier and started toward the villa, figuring she would come back for the box with her paints and art supplies. She couldn't help but wonder what Gator would have said if he knew the truth.

That she was the only witness to the cold-blooded murder of a police officer named Zeke Hartung.

Make that *missing* witness.

The story, complete with sensational headlines, had been splashed across every South Florida paper followed quickly she didn't doubt by the attack at the safe house and the death of two more officers.

As she looked up at the villa, she wondered if there was any place safe enough or far away from civilization to elude Landry Jones. If it wasn't Cape Diablo, then no place existed.

The sound of the boat's motor died off into the distance. She looked back once but the boat had already disappeared from sight. All she could see were mangrove islands on one horizon and the endless Gulf of Mexico on the other.

She couldn't remember ever feeling so isolated, so alone—not even in the middle of South Dakota, miles from the nearest town. Surely all the people looking for her would have a hard time finding her. But she didn't delude herself. She wouldn't be safe until Landry Jones was behind bars.

Willa stopped in front of the villa. She could hear the waves lapping at the dock and the wind whispering in the palms, but also the faint sound of music.

She looked up again to see an elderly woman through the sheer curtains. The woman wore a white gown and appeared to be waltzing to the music with an invisible partner.

"Hello."

Willa jumped at the sound of the male voice next to her, making her drop one of the suitcases.

"Here let me take that." He stepped around her and picked up the suitcase and reached for the second one. "I thought I heard a boat."

She could only stare at him, her heart thundering in

her chest. She'd been told there were four apartments in the villa, all vacant when she'd inquired.

"Sorry. I didn't mean to scare you," the man said. He appeared to be in his early thirties, blond, blue-eyed and tan—her original idea of what Florida men should all look like. "What's your apartment number?"

"Three."

"Then you're right up there." He pointed through an arch. She could see a wrought iron railing, a blood-red riot of bougainvillea flowers climbing the wall behind it and a weathered door with a 3 painted crudely on it.

He took the other suitcase from her and carrying both, headed through the archway into a tiled courtyard. She started to turn back to retrieve the box with her painting supplies from the dock. "I'll get that for you," he said.

Still a little unsteady after the boat ride, she decided to let him and followed him through the archway, seeing that she was right—there was a pool. Unfortunately it was dark and murky, apparently abandoned years ago but never drained.

"I'm Odell Grady," he said over his shoulder. "That's my apartment over there." He motioned across the pool to what had once been the pool house, she guessed.

"How many tenants are there?"

"Just you and me right now. Unless you count the old gal up there." He motioned to a third-floor tower section of the villa where she'd seen the woman dancing. "She's grandfathered in, so to speak."

He stopped partway up the stairs and turned to look back at her. "You were warned about her, weren't you?"

She hadn't been warned about anything except the isolation and no one to meet her at the dock, but she wasn't worried about some elderly woman who waltzed with a phantom lover. Odell was another story altogether.

"If you like peace and quiet, you definitely came to the right place," he said as he scaled the stairs. "That's why I came here. How about you?" He'd reached the landing and stopped next to one of the doors to turn to look back at her.

"Peace and quiet," she agreed as she topped the stairs. She wondered if it would be possible to get either with Odell Grady around.

He nodded, openly studying her. He had put down the suitcases just outside the door and held out his hand.

It took her a moment to realize he was waiting for the key to open her door.

"Thank you. I can take it from here."

He seemed to hesitate, then looked embarrassed. "Sorry, didn't mean to come on so strong. This place gets to you after a while. I hadn't realized what it would be like, not talking to another human being."

"How long have you been here?"

"Too long obviously. I've been talking your ear off, sorry." He stepped back, giving her space. "I'll get your other package." He turned and trotted down the stairs.

She opened the apartment door but didn't enter, instead watching him, worrying.

Odell returned with the box. "It's pretty heavy. Want me to set it inside?"

"Thank you." She let him enter but stayed outside until he'd put the box down and came back out.

He must have seen how uncomfortable she was having him in her apartment. Actually being pretty much alone on the island with him—since she doubted the elderly woman upstairs would be much help if she needed it.

"So, welcome to Cape Diablo," Odell said, dusting off his hands on his shorts. He met her gaze. He didn't look dangerous, but then she'd thought the same thing of Landry Jones, hadn't she.

"If you need anything, I'll be right down there pounding on my manual typewriter. I'm a writer," he said walking backward a few steps. "Fiction."

She relaxed a little and felt guilty for the rude way she'd reacted to his kindness.

"How about you?"

"You mean what I do for a living?" she asked, giving herself time to come up with an answer. "I've been a waitress, a barmaid, a receptionist, a grocery clerk. Right now I'm just taking a break to figure out what I want to do."

"Been there," he said. "You're still young. You'll figure it out." He cocked his head at her. "You look like an…artist to me." He must have seen her shocked expression because he laughed. "No, I'm not psychic. The box lid came open and I saw all your art supplies."

The box had come open? Not with the amount of tape she'd used. "It's just a hobby."

"Yeah, that's how my writing is. I just hope to turn it into something more," he said, and looked toward the Gulf. "This would be a great place to paint." He turned back to her. "I'd love to see your work."

"I don't let anyone see it," she said too quickly. "It's just...embarrassing at this point."

He laughed. "Probably the same reason I don't let anyone read my work." Another song drifted on the breeze. He glanced toward the third floor where the elderly woman was dancing again. "If you weren't crazy when you came here, you will be."

"I'm sorry. How long did you say you've been here?"

"Just since this afternoon, but long enough to go stir-crazy, although not as crazy as some people." He made a face and cocked his head toward the tower, making a circle with his finger next to his temple.

Since this afternoon? So he'd arrived only a little earlier than she had. She felt a chill at the thought that someone had found out where she was going and Odell had been sent to wait for her.

"Thank you again for your help."

He smiled and nodded. "My pleasure."

Almost apologetically she turned away from him. She picked up her suitcases and stepped inside the apartment. As she started to close the door, he called from the stairs, "Hey, I never caught your name."

"Will—Willie." It was out before she could call it back.

She was tired and just wanted to be left alone and she hadn't thought before she'd spoken or she would have given him the name she'd planned to use. Too late for that.

"Short for something?" he asked turning on the stairs.

She was forced back out on the balcony to keep from yelling her answer. "Actually, it's a nickname. My real name is Cara Wilson. My friends started calling me Willie and it stuck."

"Cara," he said. "That's a pretty name. But Willie suits you."

She smiled nervously and gave him a nod as she stepped back into her apartment and closed the door, leaning against it, feeling like a fool.

She concluded Odell was more lonely than anything else. *Nosy* and lonely. Unless she was wrong about him—the way she'd been wrong about Landry Jones. To think she had almost gotten in the car with Landry.

She shivered at the memory, her gaze skittering over the rooms where she'd be living until Landry was caught. The apartment wasn't bad. If you liked living in a monastery. The walls had once been painted white, the ceilings were cracked and ten feet high at least. The temperature was nice and cool, though, so that meant the walls were thick.

That was a plus and the place *was* furnished. Kinda.

Not that any of that mattered. She would be safe here. At least she prayed that was true.

Dragging her suitcases into the bedroom, she was excited to see the wonderful light coming in through the window. She felt a sense of relief. She would be able to paint in here. In fact, she couldn't wait to get started.

She dragged the box in. As she started to open it, she noticed that the tape was open on one corner and the flap turned back. She ran her finger along the edge of the tape. It had been cut.

Chapter Four

Willa's heart began to pound a little harder. Someone had cut the tape to look inside the box. Odell? Was it possible he had a knife in the pocket of his shorts? A lot of men in South Dakota carried pocket knives. But in Florida?

Or could it have been someone else? The box had been on the dock unattended for some time while Odell had brought her suitcases up to her room. But who else was there?

She glanced toward the third floor. The music had stopped again. She recalled it stopping before, a break between songs before she saw the elderly woman dancing once again. Was it possible the woman had gone down to the dock to look in Willa's belongings?

What harm could a curious old woman do anyway? Willa liked that theory better than thinking Odell had purposely cut the tape to see what was in the box. The man was nosy, but whoever had cut the box was looking for something. Looking for her?

But if whoever had looked in the box was here to kill her, then that person already knew she painted. And not even her changed appearance would fool him.

She tried to put the incident out of her mind as she unloaded her painting supplies and set up an easel by the window.

Painting relaxed her, let her escape for a while from the reality of her life, the reality that Landry Jones was still out there on the loose and she was the only witness to the murder.

Until the police captured him, she wasn't safe. Even when he was caught, she wasn't sure she would feel safe, possibly ever again.

She stacked up all of her art supplies on the top of the chest of drawers, hoping they would last until she got to leave here. Eventually she would run out of rent money and be forced to leave and get a job.

She moved to the window by the bed and peered out. Through the palms she could see the Gulf of Mexico. It looked endless. How odd not to be able to see land on the horizon. Just water as far as the eye could see. No wonder early man feared sailing to the edge and falling off.

Turning back to the room, she considered making the bed and taking a nap. She'd been running on fear for so long, she felt drained. She needed her life back. All she had to do, she told herself, was stay alive until Landry was caught.

She stared at the empty canvas on her easel. She had

to paint. It had been days since she'd gotten the opportunity. She itched to pick up a brush.

Painting had always been her survival. When her father was killed in a tractor accident. When her first love married someone else. When her mother remarried and sold the farm, hacking away the roots that had held Willa in South Dakota.

Willa hurried to catch the last of the day's light coming in through the palms. She never knew what she was going to paint until she had a brush in her hand and the white empty canvas in front of her.

To her, painting was exploration. A voyage to an unknown part of herself. Her work was a combination of what she saw and what she didn't. It was a feeling captured like a thought out of thin air.

She set up her paints and went to work, the evening light fading until she was forced to turn on a lamp. It wasn't until then that she really looked at what she'd been working on—and felt a start.

What had begun as an old building along a narrow street had turned into the street where she'd witnessed the murder. A thin slice of pale light at the back illuminated what could have been a bundle of old rags but what she knew was a body slumped against a stucco wall, the dark BMW sitting at the curb.

She stepped back from the canvas. She'd been so lost in the physical joy of painting, she hadn't even realized that she'd been reliving the murder.

From this distance, she saw the face behind the windshield of the BMW. It was subtle, almost ghostlike, but definitely a face. Landry Jones's face. The same one she'd drawn for the police. She remembered the investigators' strange reactions. When she'd asked if they knew who he was, the detective who'd been questioning her assured her they knew Landry Jones only too well.

Just her luck that a known criminal had taken an interest in her. She had wanted to ask what other crimes he'd committed but didn't want to know. Wasn't murdering a man in cold blood on a St. Pete Beach street enough?

In the painting, Landry was peering out of the darkness not at the body of the man he'd just killed—but at her. She could almost feel the heat of his dark eyes.

She stumbled back from the painting, bumping into the sagging double bed and sitting down on the bare mattress, suddenly exhausted and near tears.

Had she been foolish to think she would be safe anywhere—let alone on this island? She would always be haunted by what had happened that night, would always see Landry Jones's face, if not in her paintings then in her nightmares.

A tap at the door startled her. She didn't want to answer it but knew she couldn't pretend she'd gone out. Another tap.

"Cara? Willie?"

Odell. She groaned. Where had she come up with Cara? "Just a minute." She glanced around the room as if there might be something lying around that would give away her true identity, but didn't see anything. She couldn't help the feeling that she'd already made a mistake that was going to get her in trouble. She couldn't keep living like this.

She opened the door. "Odell," she said as if seeing him was a surprise.

"Hi. Sorry to bother you, but I noticed you didn't bring any food," he said, looking sheepish. He held out a sandwich wrapped in plastic. "If you don't want it now, you can eat it later. Turkey and cheese."

She took the sandwich. "Thank you. It looks...great." She actually smiled and he seemed to relax. A part of her felt bad about being so unfriendly. Back home in South Dakota her behavior would have been outright rude.

The whisper of fabric made them both turn. All Willa caught was a blur of white.

"She sneaks around here all the time like that, I guess," Odell said of the elderly woman who passed on the third-floor balcony overhead. "Her name's Alma Garcia. She was the nanny."

"The nanny?"

"You don't know the story of Cape Diablo?" he asked, sounding surprised. "The island is cursed. At least according to local legend. There have always been reports of strange happenings out here, including storms that wash up all kinds of interesting things. For decades it was home to pirates and treasure seekers who looted ships that sank or were sunk just off shore, smugglers and drug runners."

"Who built the villa?" she asked, unable not to. The place had drawn her from the first glimpse.

"Andres Santiago, a rather notorious pirate and smuggler, and this is where it gets interesting," Odell said, warming to his story. "Back in the late sixties, early seventies, Andres smuggled guns, drugs, anything profitable in from Central America. The Ten Thousand Islands have always been home to smugglers of all kinds because it is so remote and easy to get lost in."

She nodded remembering how quickly she'd become lost among the mangrove islands on the way here. "You said he had a nanny?"

Odell nodded. "He lived here with his wife, Medina, and three small children from his first marriage. That wife died in childbirth. Medina was the daughter of a Central American dictator. During a revolt, her father was killed but Andres managed to rescue Medina and a devoted lieutenant named Carlos Lazarro. He brought them both to the island. Carlos still lives in that old boathouse by the pier." Odell paused. "Do you really want to hear this?"

He didn't give her time to answer. But she would have said yes even if he had.

"The woman up there, Alma Garcia? She was the nanny for Andres's children." He glanced toward the third floor. Only a faint light glowed overhead. "She went crazy after what happened."

Willa felt a chill. "What *happened?*"

"First, Andres's only son drowned in the pool. Then the whole family went missing. No one ever knew what happened to them. Alma and Carlos had been inland that night. When they came home some time after midnight, they discovered everyone gone. There was blood... The authorities suspected foul play, of course, but the case was never solved. That was thirty years ago."

"How awful."

"There are lots of theories. Some say Medina's father's enemies came and killed the whole family. Others say Andres made it look as if they'd all been killed so he could disappear with his family. In Andres's will he made provisions for both Alma and Carlos to live on the island for the rest of their lives. That's why the villa was divided into apartments since the money Andres left has long since run out. A lawyer friend of the family handles everything."

Willa saw the woman sneak back into her apartment. The front of her white gown was covered with what appeared to be dirt.

"When I got here, I saw her digging," Odell said. "Local legend has it that Andres Santiago hid a small fortune on this island."

She felt her eyes widen.

Odell laughed. "If it were true, fortune hunters would have found it over the last thirty years."

"I'm surprised Alma and Carlos would want to stay here after what happened," Willa said, seeing the villa so differently now.

"I guess they had nowhere else to go. Alma spends her days creeping around here like some kind of ghost. Carlos is the caretaker but most of the time from what

I can tell, he's on the other side of the island in his boat fishing." He seemed to notice that she was still holding her sandwich. "You probably want to get that in the fridge and I've talked your ear off again. Sorry."

"No, I enjoyed hearing the story, and thank you for the sandwich."

He smiled. "Holler if you need anything. And don't worry about Alma and Carlos. They seem harmless enough."

"Thanks." Willa stepped back into her apartment and closed the door. She waited a few moments, until she heard Odell's footfalls retreat, before she locked the door.

After she put the sandwich in the fridge, she dragged her suitcase over to the marred old chest of drawers and unpacked. At the bottom of her suitcase, she found the sheets and towels she'd brought. She made the bed and hung up the towels in the bathroom, surprised to see there was a huge clawfoot tub.

Some of her fatigue evaporated at the thought of sinking neck-deep into a tub of hot water scented with her favorite bath soap. She popped in the plug and turned on the water. The old pipes groaned and complained but after a few moments, wonderfully warm water began to fill the tub.

Quickly she checked to make sure she'd locked the door before she went back to the bathroom and stripped off her clothing and stepped into the tub.

Everything was going to be all right, she told herself as she immersed herself in the warm water and began to soap her body in the rich lather. From somewhere she heard music again, the song older than the woman on the third floor. Past the music, she heard voices, though too faint to make out the words.

She couldn't help but think about the story Odell had told her. The history of Cape Diablo and the Santiago family fascinated her. She'd felt something when she'd stepped off the boat and looked up at the crumbling old villa. A sense of mystery. A story unfolding. Or had she sensed something else? The spirits of the lost souls? Or a sense of foreboding as if she'd been drawn to this island for another purpose?

She shivered, wondering again what could have happened to the family and even more intrigued by the woman who'd stayed on upstairs.

Odell certainly was knowledgeable about Cape Diablo. She felt foolish for suspecting him of having other motives for being on the island. And yet, anyone could learn the history of the place. And pretending to be a writer gave him the perfect cover.

She shook her head at the path her mind had taken. She hated that she was suspicious of everyone now.

Finishing her bath, she toweled dry and dressed in a sleeveless nightshirt. She felt better, calmer, back in control somewhat, she thought as she started to wipe the steam from the mirror and was momentarily startled by her own unfamiliar image in the glass.

Her hand went to her short curly auburn hair. It did make her eyes seem larger. Or that could have been the fear.

She picked up the glasses from where she'd left them on the sink. The lenses were clear, but the plastic frames distracted from her face enough to make her look entirely different from the woman she'd been just weeks before.

She touched her hair again, missing the feel of her long, naturally straight blond hair inherited from her Swedish ancestors.

But she would let her hair grow out again. After Landry was caught, after the trial—when it was safe to go back to her life, she told herself, trying hard to believe she could ever reclaim it.

Glancing around the apartment, she decided the first item of business would be to make this place more her own. What little furniture there was had been shoved against each wall.

She grabbed the end of the couch and pulled it away from the wall and saw at once why it had been pushed against the wall as it had been.

There was a sizable hole in the wall behind it.

On closer inspection, she saw that the hole—four inches wide, a good foot high and seemingly endless in depth—had been chipped into the adobe wall. She couldn't tell how deep it ran. Not without a flashlight.

As she straightened she noticed a scrap of paper on the floor near the hole. She picked it up and saw that it was a piece of a torn photograph. The piece appeared to be part of a face covered with something like a gauzy veil or a film of some kind.

She peered into the hole and thought she saw another piece of the torn photograph. How odd.

Vaulting over the couch she dug in her purse for the penlight on her key ring. In the kitchen she found a butter knife and returned to behind the couch.

Shining the tiny light into the hole, she began to dig out the pieces of the photo with the butter knife. She still couldn't tell how deep the hole was—obviously too deep for her dim light. But there were more pieces of the photograph in there, as if they'd fallen down from the floor above.

Diligently she worked the pieces out until she couldn't reach any more.

Just as she was starting to collect the scraps, a sliver of light sliced down through the top of the hole. Willa angled her gaze upward into the opening and saw light coming through what appeared to be a crack in floor-boards upstairs.

She'd thought no one lived directly above her. She heard the creak of footsteps on the floor overhead. The light went out. She listened, but heard nothing more.

Taking the pieces of the photograph over to the small kitchen table, she pulled up a chair and began to fit the pieces together like a puzzle, curious after seeing the veiled face in the first piece.

The graphic artist who'd mentioned Cape Diablo had also been an avid photographer. Was it possible this was one of her photos? Or maybe that she'd even stayed in this very room?

The photograph began to take shape. Several of the edge pieces were missing but she was starting to see an image. What was it she was looking at?

She laid down the last piece and felt a jolt. It was a photo of the pool in the courtyard, the water murky and dark.

Funny, but the face that had spurred her curiosity enough to put the photograph back together in the first place seemed to have disappeared.

That was strange.

Carefully she turned the pieces of the photograph a hundred and eighty degrees and gasped.

A boy of about four was lying on the bottom of the pool in the deep end, the dark water like a mask over his face. There was no doubt that the child was dead.

Chapter Five

Abruptly Willa shoved back her chair and stumbled to her feet. Odell had said Andres Santiago's only son had died here. Drowned in the pool? But that had been more than thirty years ago.

Her hands were shaking. How long had this photo been in the wall? If the shot had been taken by her friend, then it would have been just weeks ago.

Suddenly scared, Willa looked at the photograph again.

The body on the bottom of the pool was gone. So was the little boy's terrified face.

She stared down at the photograph. Had she just imagined seeing the little boy? Could it have been a trick of the light? Or just her imagination after the terrible story Odell had told her?

She glanced toward the hole in the wall. But if it had just been a photograph of the murky pool, then why had someone torn the photograph into tiny pieces then hidden them in the wall?

Unable to suppress a shudder, Willa thought of the woman on the third floor and the light that had bled down from overhead as the woman moved around up there. Alma Garcia. She'd been the child's nanny, Willa thought as her stomach knotted. Had she been caring for the little boy the day he drowned?

Willa glanced again at the photo, telling herself it was just a photograph of the pool. Nothing more.

Shivering from a nonexistent cold breeze that seemed to have crept into the room, Willa scooped up the pieces of photograph and dumped them into the trash can. She couldn't keep seeing death everywhere she looked.

The curtains billowed in at the window, startling her. The tropical breeze was warm. The chill gone from the room again.

She stepped to the window, surprised how quickly it had gotten dark. Through the palms, she could see the lights of a boat far out on the dark horizon. Below her, shadows moved restlessly across the courtyard. She could smell salt in the air coming in from the Gulf, hear the breeze rustling the palm fronds.

The music had stopped. She realized the voices she'd heard were coming from the other side of the villa behind her. Moving to the back of her small apartment, she opened the window as quietly as possible.

Two people were talking beneath the window in a low murmur. She couldn't make out their words. As her eyes adjusted to the darkness she could however make out two figures in the shadow of the house.

As they moved, Willa saw that one was wearing an old-fashioned white gown like she'd seen the nanny wearing earlier while dancing. The other figure was that of a man. He too was older, his voice sounding gravelly.

He appeared to be trying to persuade the woman to go with him somewhere. After a moment they parted, the woman slipping through an archway back into the villa. The elderly man faded into the darkness and vegetation of the island as if he'd never existed.

The man must have been Carlos Lazarro, she realized who, according to Odell, lived in the old boathouse.

Willa closed the window and started to close the blinds as well, when something caught her eye. Movement. The old man? Had he come back? She watched someone moving through the vegetation, but it was too dark to make out who it was. Not the old man. The person moved too easily. Almost catlike, making little sound, the movement fluid and hinting of power. Whoever it was headed for the back of the villa.

Landry Jones.

Willa shook off the thought. Landry couldn't have found her. It had to be Odell. She moved to the door, unlocked it and stepped out onto the long balcony over the courtyard. Below her, the pool was cloudy and bottomless. She stared down into it, seeing nothing and glad of it.

As she glanced across the courtyard toward Odell's apartment, she saw that a single light shone through the cracks between the blinds in what she assumed was his living room. The window was open. She listened for the clack of an old manual typewriter, but there was no sound coming from his apartment.

But behind the house she could hear the purr of a motor. The generator that supplied the electricity. They'd had a generator on the farm for when bad weather took out their power lines. She knew the sound well growing up on the South Dakota prairie.

She moved away from her open apartment door, sneaking as quietly as possible along the balcony to the back wall of the villa to gaze out through the thick foliage in the direction where she'd seen the person going. No one. Could it have been an animal? Whatever it had been it certainly moved like one.

Another rhythmic sound drew her attention. She moved along the back of the second-story walkway away from her apartment. Through the trees she spotted a figure bent over digging a hole in the ground. The sound of the steady scrape of a shovel blade through the soil drifted on the night breeze.

As the figure straightened, she saw that it was Odell. Of course that was who she'd seen from the window, she thought with a wave of relief. He turned up another shovelful of dirt, stopped and looked back toward the villa as if he'd heard something. Or sensed her watching him.

She melted back into the dark shadows along the wall, hoping he hadn't seen her spying on him. What could he be digging up? Or was he burying something?

He resumed his digging but she stayed hidden, afraid

he would look over his shoulder again and see her. The shoveling stopped, then resumed again.

She took a peek. He seemed to be covering up the hole now. She watched as he patted down the disturbed ground then covered it with several palm fronds.

As he started toward the villa, she flattened herself against the wall, not daring to move. She feared he would see her even in the dark shadows because of the light-colored nightshirt she wore. But he didn't look up in her direction. He seemed intent on hurrying back to his apartment.

She watched him come through an archway almost hidden by vegetation and keep to the shadows, not making a sound as he entered his apartment. He no longer had the shovel. Nor was he carrying anything she could see.

Willa stood there until he'd closed his apartment door. Another light came on deeper in the apartment, then went out. What was all that about?

Did she even want to know? For just an instant, she thought about sneaking down there and finding out. Wouldn't she sleep better if she did?

Yeah, right.

She shivered as she made her way back to her open apartment door. Slipping inside, she locked the door behind her.

Whatever it was Odell had dug up or buried, it was none of her business. Though it was odd. And even a little chilling.

As she padded barefoot toward her bedroom she

caught an unfamiliar scent in the air and slowed. Perfume? It smelled like...gardenias? Had someone been in her apartment? She'd foolishly left the door wide open and hadn't been paying any attention during the time she'd been watching Odell.

Deeper into the apartment, the scent grew stronger then faded all together as if she'd only imagined it. Like she'd imagined the little boy's face in the photo?

She stopped in the middle of her bedroom. Her pulse jumped, her heart leaping to her throat. Someone had been in her apartment. She hadn't imagined the scent of gardenias and what she saw—or in this case didn't see.

Her easel stood empty.

The painting she'd done of Landry Jones and the murder was gone.

Trembling, Willa removed the shade from the lamp on the table next to the bed and hefting the base, quickly searched the small apartment to make sure the thief wasn't still there.

The apartment was small with few places to hide. Once she'd checked the bathroom and the closet and under the bed, that didn't leave much of a hiding place.

But still she moved the couch out away from the wall to look behind it, feeling foolish. Why would someone be hiding in the apartment after taking the painting? But why would anyone come into her apartment and take an unfinished painting to begin with?

Once she was sure there was no one lurking in the

apartment, she put the lamp back beside her bed, the shade on again and turned on all the lights.

Her stomach felt queasy and she remembered the sandwich Odell had given her. The supply boat wouldn't be coming until tomorrow morning with her groceries.

She had bought a box of granola bars before she'd met Gator at the dock and several bottles of water. She took the water from her large purse, opened one and put the other in the fridge. Too antsy to sit, she ate the sandwich and one of the bars standing up.

She felt a bit better but still nervous as she listened to the sounds of the night and the creaks and groans of the old villa and thought of the story about the Santiago family. Overhead, she heard footfalls on the floor as if someone was creeping around up there, then silence.

On impulse, she checked the hole behind the couch. No light shone from the floor above. She slid the couch back, double-checked the door to make sure it was locked, then made sure all the windows were closed and locked before hooking a chair under the doorknob as an extra precaution before going to bed.

As exhausted as she was, she thought sleep would elude her, especially given that someone had taken the disturbing painting she'd planned to paint over in the morning. Who? And why? Alma Garcia? The same person who'd cut the tape on the painting supply box while it was on the dock? Maybe the poor old soul had a problem with taking things. Willa would have to keep her door locked. And keep an eye on the old woman.

And Odell. What had he buried? Or dug up? She knew she would have to find out. She thought about going out there now but suddenly she couldn't keep her eyes open. Sleep dragged her down as if she'd been drugged.

She tried to fight it, suddenly afraid that Odell had put something in the sandwich. She felt as if she were underwater desperately trying to swim to the surface. She thought she heard a sound at her door then someone calling her name but then she went under and there was nothing but blackness.

In the dream the water was dark. She stood on the edge of the pool. There was something just below the surface. She could almost make out what it was. She leaned closer.

A face began to take shape. The face of a little boy like the one she'd seen in the photograph except the boy seemed to be fighting to save himself, as if he was being held under. There was terror in his eyes and he was gasping.

Suddenly the child's face floated to the surface. Not the face of a little boy but the bloated, distended face of a monster, the decomposed skin slipping off, the face literally dissolving before her eyes.

Willa screamed and lurched backward but the child's hand came out of the fetid water and grabbed her wrist, pulling her toward the pool as if to drag her to the bottom with him.

Frantically she fought to free herself but the grip on her wrist was like a steel band. She screamed again as she was dragged to the lip of the pool, what was left of the child's face grinning grotesquely up at her.

"Hey! It's me!"

Suddenly her eyes flew open and she fell backward. Odell grabbed her and pulled her back from the edge of the pool. She struck out at him, still deep in the nightmare.

"Hey, what's wrong with you?"

He held her at arm's length until her eyes focused on him, then he let go. She stumbled back from him, confused and shaking with terror.

"Are you all right?"

She blinked and looked around, memory of where she was slowly coming back to her. "How did I get down here?"

He shook his head. "Oh, man, were you sleepwalking?"

Her gaze flickered over the moonlit courtyard. Still in the grip of the dream, she stared at the dark water of the pool, until she finally pulled her gaze away and looked at Odell. He was wearing only pajama bottoms, his chest and feet bare, hair mussed as if he'd just woken up.

"I heard a scream and I came running out...." He was staring at her, looking almost as scared of her as she was of him. "That was really creepy. I've never seen anyone sleepwalking before. You were looking right at me and yet you didn't seem to be seeing me at all. If I hadn't grabbed you, you looked like you were going to fall into the deep end of the pool."

She tried to make sense of what he was saying. "It was only a dream?"

He chuckled, looking relieved that she was no longer freaking. "More like a nightmare from the way you were screaming."

It had been so *real.* She shot a glance toward the stagnant water of the pool again and shuddered, hugging her bare arms. She glanced down and saw that her feet were bare and realized she was wearing only her nightshirt. Although it covered her from her shoulders to her knees, she felt half-naked in the hot humid night air with this man.

She remembered the sandwich and the feeling that she'd been drugged. Was it possible he'd put something in the sandwich to make her hallucinate? But why would he do that? If he'd been sent here to kill her, why not just drown her in the pool get it over with? Why save her?

"Are you sure you're all right?" Odell asked.

She nodded, realizing that the last time she'd gotten even a little close to a stranger had colored her thinking. She used to be so trusting. But Landry Jones had changed all that.

Thoughts of what could have happened if she'd gotten into the car with Landry that night skittered past. Another shudder ran through her as she stepped farther away from Odell.

"If you're all right, I'm going back to bed," he said, seeing her move away from him. He seemed irritated. After all, according to him, he'd just saved her.

She nodded and stumbled backward to the stairs, groping with one hand behind her as if blind, even though an almost full moon and a canopy of stars now lit the courtyard.

Odell said nothing, just watched her until she disappeared up the steps and through the open door of her apartment. She closed the door, locked it and moved to the window to peer through the blinds down on the courtyard and the pool. Had it really only been a nightmare?

Odell was still standing by the pool looking up at her apartment.

She retreated from the window, letting the blind fall back into place. She couldn't quit shaking. She hadn't walked in her sleep since she was a child.

Shuddering again at the memory of the child's face in the water, she hurried to turn on a lamp, sending the darkness skittering back to the far corners of the apartment. But no light could take away the chill the nightmare had left behind. Or rid her of the feeling that it hadn't been a dream at all.

The hand coming out of the pool had been Andres Santiago's dead son grabbing her—

Almost as if still asleep, she slowly looked down at her left wrist, not realizing until that moment that she'd been rubbing it.

A stifled cry escaped her lips. The skin was chafed red where something—someone—had grabbed her wrist, the skin already starting to bruise.

Chapter Six

Willa woke to the sound of a boat motor. She bolted upright in bed, momentarily confused. All the lights were on in her apartment and she realized she'd left them on all night. She was on top of the covers where she must have lain once she'd returned to her apartment last night.

Her memory was fuzzy. Had she dreamt all of it, including waking up by the pool? She looked down at her wrist, shocked again to see distinct bruises in the shape of fingertips. And calluses on her palms from shoveling.

She groaned. Some of it had definitely been real.

Last night she knew she wouldn't be able to get back to sleep until she found out if Odell had buried something behind the villa.

She'd waited until his lights went out, and then giving another thirty minutes to make sure everything was quiet in the villa, she dressed and sneaked down.

As she passed the pool, she hadn't dared look into

the water as if it might cast a spell on her. Or even worse, that she might see the little boy and he might reach for her again as he'd done in the nightmare.

Past the pool, she'd slipped through the arch, just as Odell had done earlier. The moon had sent silver shafts of light down through the palms and dense vegetation close to the villa. Just as she'd suspected, Odell had left the shovel just outside the courtyard leaning against the wall.

Silently she took it and gazed into the darkness under the trees for the spot where she'd seen him digging. It was harder to find from this angle. But she was good with directions. It went with being raised in South Dakota. A person could get lost on the prairie with no trees or even a knoll to use as a marker.

A few yards from the villa, the darkness settled over her like a shroud. She stumbled to the spot and turned to look back at the villa.

No lights shone. Moonlight played along the edge of the back wall. She saw no dark figure watching her, heard nothing as she turned back to the spot and removed the palm fronds Odell had used to cover it.

The earth had obviously been turned here. She was more than having second thoughts as she took the shovel in her hands and began to dig. While she'd brought the penlight, she didn't want to use it unless she absolutely had to, fearing that the light might be seen from the villa. The last thing she needed was an audience for what she suspected would be one of her more foolish acts.

She tried to imagine what her friends back in South

Dakota would say if they could see her now. Worse, her mother. Better to think about that instead of what she might be digging up.

The blade struck something, making a ringing sound that seemed too loud. Everyone back at the villa had to have heard. Worse, she started to imagine all kinds of things buried down there. She shuddered and carefully turned over another shovelful then another.

Something glittered in the dim light. She put down the shovel and, taking a chance, turned on the penlight and shone it down into the hole, her nerves on end.

What the heck? She bent closer. It appeared to be a pint jar full of something. She cringed, not wanting to pick it up and yet how could she not? As if she could just cover it back up now…

Gingerly she bent down and cautiously picked up the jar wondering why Odell would have gone to the trouble to bury it. In the glow of the penlight, she could now see that it was a small mayonnaise jar and it was full of nails and tacks, all swimming in a yellowish liquid. Talk about odd.

She tilted the jar, the contents rattling softly. This made no sense. Putting down the penlight, she tried the lid. It unscrewed easily. Bracing herself, she took a whiff and recoiled at the smell. It couldn't be! But she knew it was. The color. The smell.

She quickly screwed the lid back on and returned the jar to the hole. It didn't take long to rebury it. She tamped down the earth and then covered the spot with the palm fronds. Carrying the shovel, she walked back to the villa, watching to make sure no one had seen her. She felt like a fool.

After leaning the shovel against the wall where she'd found it, she returned to her apartment, washed her hands and changed back into her nightgown.

It wasn't until she climbed back into bed that she let herself think about what she'd discovered. Odell had filled a jar with sharp objects and urinated on them, then sealed up the jar and buried it outside the villa.

It was a talisman. Willa knew because of an old woman who lived down the road from her family's former farm when she was a kid. The woman lived alone and some people said she was a witch. She was always brewing up herbs and poultices. The one time Willa had been in the woman's house she'd seen books about spells and hexes—and ways to protect yourself against evil. One required burying a jar filled with sharp objects and urine in the backyard to keep you safe from anything—or anyone who might want to hurt you.

What did Odell Grady need to protect himself against? The evil of the house? Or the evil he was about to do?

Willa's head ached. She couldn't be sure if it was from a fitful night of sleep or being drugged. She'd been a fool to eat the sandwich, knowing that Odell Grady might be a hired killer who'd been sent to make sure she never testified against Landry Jones.

But would Landry Jones send someone to kill her? Or would he come himself?

The thought sent a shudder through her as she quickly dressed to meet the supply boat, reminding herself that if Odell was a hired killer, he certainly hadn't acted like one last night.

He could have drowned her. Or poisoned her. He had done neither. In fact, if he was telling the truth, he'd saved her from the pool. Wasn't it possible that she really had been walking in her sleep, dreaming about that torn-up photograph, thinking she saw a body at the bottom of the pool?

But that didn't explain why he'd buried a talisman against evil behind the villa. Hadn't Gator said people came to Cape Diablo because they were running from something? Maybe someone was after Odell Grady.

The sound of the boat motor grew louder. Hurriedly she opened her door on the beautiful Florida sunny day and took a deep breath of the salty air. On impulse, she decided to get rid of the trash on her way. She didn't want that stupid photograph in her apartment. The last thing she needed was another nightmare like last night.

But as she picked up the small trash basket, she saw with a start that it was empty. Had she taken it out last night?

Not that she remembered.

She glanced toward her empty easel. Had the scraps of photograph gone the way of the missing painting?

The boat motor grew even louder. She put down the trash basket, not even wanting to contemplate why whoever had taken her painting would have also taken the scraps of a photo of nothing more than a murky pool.

As she rushed down to the dock, the supply boat came into view. She was half hoping it was Gator. But as the boat came closer, she saw that the driver was a stranger and he wasn't alone. There were two others in the boat with him, both women. Visitors? Or new tenants?

"Good morning." Odell came up behind her, keeping a little distance between them as if wary of her after last night.

"Mornin'," she said, embarrassed. If he was telling the truth, he'd saved her from possibly drowning in that gross pool last night and she hadn't even thanked him. In fact, she'd been rude to him. "About last night…thanks."

"No problem."

At the memory she looked down at her wrist and saw the bruises where fingers had pressed into her flesh.

"Oh no. I hurt you," Odell said, sounding horrified as he grabbed her hand and turned her hand palm up to look at the bruises on her wrist. He grimaced. "I'm sorry. You were just pulling so hard. I couldn't let go and let you fall into that pool. In the state you were in I was afraid you would have drowned or at least died of something after being in that putrid water."

She had to smile. "I appreciate you not letting that happen." But the suspicious part of her mind still wondered if he was telling the truth.

"I'm just glad you were there," she said, reverting to

the manners she'd been taught. "Thank you. I was so upset last night. I'm sorry if I seemed ungrateful."

He smiled. "I'm glad I could be of help. It must have been some nightmare."

She nodded.

Odell looked past her, his expression brightening. "Wow."

Just then the supply boat banged into the dock. Odell righted her as the dock rocked, then grabbed the bow of the boat to steady it. "Good morning," he said with much more enthusiasm than he'd shown her.

The greeting, she saw wasn't for the supply boat driver, who must be Bull. He was a younger version of Gator, although just as weather-beaten and no more friendly.

No, what had brightened Odell was the tall redheaded woman in short shorts and an even snugger red halter top. Thirty-something, the redhead could have been a model. The other passenger in the boat was apparently a teenager. The girl had the sullen Goth look going: her eyes rimmed with black, her nose, eyebrow and lower lip pierced, along with her ears, and her dyed black hair stringy and in her eyes. She wore black jeans and a black crocheted top that revealed a lot of sunless white skin and a black bra.

Willa's first thought was that the girl must be roasting in this heat dressed like that. She had a bored, annoyed expression as she ignored Odell's offer of a hand out and agilely stepped to the dock.

"You have got to be kidding," the teenager said as she looked toward the villa with disdain.

Meanwhile, the redhead smiled up at Odell as she took his hand and awkwardly stepped from the boat. The redhead stumbled into Odell. He caught her, his arms coming around her waist to steady her.

Willa rolled her eyes. The woman couldn't have been more obvious if she tried. And Odell... What a chivalrous guy, Willa thought, watching the little scene. First he'd rescued Willa last night. Or so he'd said. And now he was playing knight in armor to what appeared to be their new neighbor, if the three matching red suitcases were any indication.

The breeze picked up a few notes from an old classic song and Willa turned to glance back at the deteriorated Spanish villa. On the third floor, the elderly woman looked out, then the curtain fall back into place. Willa would bet the woman smelled of gardenias.

"Odell Grady," she heard Mr. Chivalrous say to the redhead. "Welcome to Cape Diablo."

The woman gave him a demure nod as she stepped out of his arms, but not far. "Henrietta LaFrance, but my friends all call me Henri." She favored Willa with a glance.

"This is Cara," Odell said. "Or do you prefer Willie?"

Henrietta cocked her head. "You look more like a Willie not a Cara."

So she'd heard. "Willie is fine." She knew she would never remember to answer to Cara anyway and now wished she hadn't mentioned the other name.

Odell hurried to tie up the boat and help unload all of the supplies, including the three large red suitcases and two large army-green duffel bags that apparently belonged to Goth Girl.

Mother and daughter? Henri didn't look like the mother type. Nor had Willa seen the two women exchange even a look, let alone a word. So did this mean that they had come out to rent the remaining two apartments?

It seemed odd that when Willa had called, all the apartments had been vacant and now were rented. Maybe that was normal. Still, it made her a little anxious. At least the two new renters were women, though Willa couldn't imagine what had brought either of them to Cape Diablo. Henri looked like a woman who would have been happier at Club Med. And Goth Girl didn't look like she'd be happy anywhere.

"I'll get that," Odell said when Willa reached for the box of supplies with her apartment number on it.

"I've got it." She softened her words. "Thanks, but it's not heavy. Anyway, Henrietta needs your help more than I do."

"Henri," the redhead corrected. "Thanks," she said as Odell attempted to carry all three of her heavy suitcases. Henri took the smaller one from him and they started toward the villa.

Goth Girl made a face at their backs, slung a duffel bag strap over each shoulder and followed at a distance.

Bull was watching Henri walk away. He hadn't said a word but what he was thinking was all too evident in his expression, especially the slack jaw.

"Is this customary?" she asked him.

He looked up at her as if seeing her for the first time. "What?"

"This many tenants."

He frowned. "People come and go. Right now they're all coming. Don't understand the attraction, though," he said, glancing toward the old villa. "That one won't stay long," he said, no doubt meaning the redhead. "Few do. Nothing to do here even if the place wasn't cursed."

"Cursed?" she asked, curious if he would tell her something different from what Odell had.

He didn't bother to look at her. "You really don't know? Ask Odell. He's writing a book about the place."

She frowned. That might explain then why he knew so much about Cape Diablo and the Santiago family.

Willa forced Bull to redirect his attention for a few minutes as she paid for her supplies and placed her order for the next week.

"How was your first night on the island?" Bull asked, shading his eyes to study her.

"Fine," she said a little too quickly.

He chuckled and pocketed her money and her list for next week's supplies. "I guess those dark circles under your eyes could be from staying up all night with Odell." He chuckled at his own joke. "He doesn't seem your type, though."

What did that mean?

Odell and Henri were headed back to the dock for the rest of the load.

"See you next week then." Bull seemed to hesitate. "I guess Gator told you that if anything happens that you decide you don't want to stay here, you can get Carlos, you know the old fisherman who lives in the boathouse, to take you to the mainland if you are in trouble. He's okay."

She wanted to ask him more, like what kind of "trouble" he might be referring to, and if Carlos was "okay," was Odell not? But Henri and Odell had returned to pick up the supply boxes. "Thanks" was all she said to Bull. At least there was a way off the island in a hurry if she needed it. And for some reason, both Bull and Gator seemed to think she might need it.

Feeling uneasy, she watched Bull take off in the boat. Both men seemed worried about her—and neither even knew just how much trouble she was in. Within seconds the boat disappeared into the line of green mangrove islands and was gone.

Henri and Odell came back down to the dock to help with the rest of the supply boxes. Both were talking as if they were old friends. Maybe they were, Willa thought. Maybe nothing was as it seemed. Was Odell writing a book about Cape Diablo and what had happened here? If so, why didn't he just say so? She watched Henri and Odell, both lost in conversation, pick up the remainder of their items from the dock and leave. Willa waited as she saw Goth Girl coming back down. The girl looked surlier than before, if that was possible.

"Hi, I'm Willie," Willa said, catching herself before she blurted out her real name. She held out her hand.

The girl just stared at it, but mumbled the word "Blossom." Goth Girl had one of those young faces that made it hard to gauge her age. The eyes had an old look, as if the girl had seen way too much during her short lifetime, Willa thought. Willa's heart went out to her. She knew firsthand what it was like to age almost overnight after witnessing something horrendous.

"Blossom. That's a unique name," Willa said, trying to be friendly and at the same time wondering what the girl was doing here. Blossom obviously wasn't pleased to be here.

"Blossom is my stage name," she said with a roll of her eyes. "Don't tell me you've never heard of me."

Willa wouldn't dare. She understood stage names. Like Cara was hers.

"You've never heard of me," Blossom accused with obvious contempt. "I've only like done a ton of films, plays and commercials. Are you one of those freaks who doesn't watch TV?"

"I've been too busy to watch much TV," Willa said, deciding befriending this girl had been a mistake. "So what brings you to Cape Diablo?"

Blossom made a face. "My agent, the bitch. She thinks I need a break. She just can't stand the idea of me having any fun. I'm just supposed to make money for her and my parents. They're in on it, too, the parasites. They all think my friends are dragging me down."

The girl looked even younger as tears welled in her eyes. "A week. I have to spend a frigging week here. It's blackmail. I should have them arrested. I can't wait until I'm old enough to dump them all."

Still feeling the effects of the headache she'd awakened with, Willa couldn't think of a thing to say as the girl spun around, picked up her supply box and headed for the villa.

After a moment, Willa picked up her own supply box from the dock again and followed. Avoiding the sour girl wouldn't be difficult and now that Odell had Henri to talk to, Willa wouldn't have anyone to bother her. She hurried back to her apartment, anxious to have some breakfast and start painting.

As she climbed the stairs, she could hear Henri's and Odell's voices in the apartment below her but couldn't make out the words. Blossom disappeared into a small apartment at the end under Willa's bedroom. Willa realized there were two small studios under her larger apartment. She'd been lucky to get the rental, it appeared.

After unpacking her food supplies, she made herself breakfast and went right to work painting. It surprised her sometimes how the paintings came to her. She worked furiously caught up in the process, hardly paying any attention to what began to appear on the canvas.

She wasn't sure how much time had passed when she heard voices in the courtyard. She stepped back from the easel to stare at what she'd painted. The villa, the walls cloaked in what appeared to be a bright red spray of bougainvillea. She stared at the painting, disturbed by the feeling it gave her.

Leaving the painting and the uneasy feeling it gave her, her thoughts returned to what Bull had said about Cape Diablo being cursed—and Odell writing a book about it. Unconsciously she massaged the bruises on her wrist.

She could still hear Odell downstairs with Henri. Glancing out the window, she saw that he'd left his door open. She could see a small desk with a typewriter right by the door. This might be her only chance.

Shocked by what she was about to do, Willa slipped out of her apartment and sneaked down the stairs and across the courtyard. She didn't look into the depths of the pool as she passed it. Nor did she turn to glance back until she reached the pool house and Odell's apartment.

The blinds in Henri's apartment were drawn. Willa could hear Henri laughing, as if she found Odell highly amusing. Which made Willa suspicious. But then she was suspicious of everyone, wasn't she?

Taking another quick look back at Henri's apartment to make sure no one had come out or was watching through the blinds, Willa stepped through Odell's open doorway.

It took a moment for her eyes to adjust in the cool darkness inside the apartment. She moved to the desk. Next to the old-fashioned manual typewriter was a ream of white paper that had yet to be opened. On the other side was a stack of newspapers.

Her heart jumped as she saw the newspapers. Some were yellowed with age and felt brittle in her fingers.

She read the headline on the top one. Entire Family Disappears From Cape Diablo.

So Bull had been right apparently.

As she set the newspaper gingerly back down, she saw a more recent headline on a paper below it.

All breath rushed from her. She lifted the older newspaper and pulled out the more recent one and gasped.

Next to the headline, Key Witness Missing In Murder Of Undercover Cop: Hunt On Following Safe House Attack, was her photo.

Chapter Seven

Willa grabbed the edge of the desk, her knees going weak as she stared at the photograph of her escaping the safe house. How had anyone gotten this? But she knew. It had to have been taken from one of the media helicopters.

She remembered one of the officers guarding her had called for backup just a few seconds after the safe house was attacked. The media must have picked up the call on the scanner.

She stared at the photo, her heart sinking. Vaguely she recalled looking up and seeing a helicopter overhead as she was running away. She'd thought it was the police and had kept running, acutely aware that the police couldn't protect her from the likes of Landry Jones or the men he worked for.

The shot of her had been blown up, the picture grainy, but even with her hair no longer long and straight and blond, she had no trouble recognizing herself.

Had Odell recognized her?

She tried not to panic. On impulse she took the section with her photo and the story about Zeke Hartung's murder, quickly folded it and stuffed it under the waistband of her shorts, covering it with her shirt.

The rest of the paper she would leave. She started to slide it back into the spot where she'd found it then noticed there was a laptop computer under his desk. Was the old manual typewriter just for show?

"You a news junkie, too?" Odell asked from his apartment doorway.

She jumped and spun around to face him, the newspaper still in her hands, her mind racing for an explanation for being in his apartment.

"The door was open," she managed to say. She'd left it open on purpose so she would hear him coming. But she'd been so upset and busy trying to get the newspaper back in the right place that she *hadn't* heard him. How long had he been standing there watching her? Had he seen her take the front page and hide it under her shirt?

"I can do without a lot but not the news," Odell said, leaning against the doorjamb watching her. "I have to know what's happening back on the mainland. You're welcome to read that paper if you'd like. I'm finished with it."

She looked down at the newspaper in her hand and said the first thing that came to mind. "I was just checking my horoscope."

He smiled. "You do that, too? It's silly but I can't help

myself. When I spill salt, I have to toss some of it over my left shoulder." He smiled. "I even knock on wood. Silly, huh?"

"No. We all have our own superstitions," she said, remembering what he'd buried behind the villa. "If you don't mind, I will take the newspaper. Might as well read 'Dear Abby' while I'm at it."

He wasn't looking at her but at his typewriter now. She hadn't noticed that there was a sheet of white paper sticking out of it. When she'd seen the ream of unopened paper she'd assumed he hadn't been writing yet.

She could almost read what he'd typed—

He stepped to her, blocking her view of the typewriter. "I'm glad you were just after the newspaper and not trying to read what I'd written on my book." His smile didn't seem to reach his eyes now.

She smiled, hers even more strained. "Okay, you caught me. I was curious. Bull said you were writing a book on Cape Diablo."

Odell laughed. "I should have known he would blab. Okay, now you know. I'm fictionalizing it since no one knows what really happened, except maybe that old woman upstairs or her boyfriend, the Ancient Mariner, as I call him. But neither of them is talking. At least not to anyone but themselves," he added, and laughed at his own joke.

"I'm sure the book will be a bestseller."

"You think?" He seemed to relax a little.

She nodded, still smiling. She wanted to ask him

what had him so scared that he was worried about evil curses. She wanted to go back to her apartment. She could feel the newspaper article under her shirt growing damp against her bare skin.

"Well, thanks for the newspaper," she said, holding it against her chest. She started to step away and heard the crinkle of the newspaper article she'd hidden under her T-shirt.

"Hey," Odell said.

She froze.

"You'd better watch the sun as fair as your skin is," he said, eyeing her. "You look flushed and a little unsteady on your feet. The sun and heat on this island will do a fair-skinned girl like you right in."

Or something would, she thought.

"You're obviously not from Florida," he said. "Some place up north?"

She could feel him studying her. Had he seen the resemblance to the page one photo of her? She hadn't had time to read the story and see if it mentioned her name or that she was from South Dakota. No doubt the police had been forced to be forthcoming after two of their officers had been gunned down at the safe house and the media had photos.

"No, actually I was born and raised here," she lied. "I just avoid the sun."

"Probably a good idea," he agreed, sounding like he knew she was lying. "You must have gone to a good college. No Floridian accent like most of us. But some accent I haven't been able to place yet." He was no longer smiling.

"I think I'll lie down for a while." She started for the stairs, feeling his gaze drilling into her back as she hugged the newspaper to her stomach and practically ran to get away.

"If you're really interested in the book I'm working on, maybe we could get together and talk about the ghosts that haunt this island," he called after her.

"What ghosts?" Henri said, sticking her head out the open door of her apartment as Willa ran up the stairs.

"Cape Diablo ghosts," Odell said with a chuckle. "Has to be told over a good bottle of wine, though."

"I have the wine," Henri offered. "What do you say, Willie?"

Willa had reached her apartment, opened the door and was almost safely inside. Just not quick enough. She thought of several reasons to decline as she looked down and saw Odell watching her, waiting.

"That is unless Willie is too scared," he said, as if trying to make it sound as if he was joking. His gaze met hers.

"I'm not afraid of ghosts," she said, meeting his eyes.

Odell lifted a brow. "Great. Later I'll get the barbecue grill going. We'll make it a party."

"You got yourself a date," Henri said.

"Sounds great," Willa agreed, just to be agreeable. She would come up with an excuse later.

She closed her door, heard the music coming from the third floor again and shivered as she remembered her stolen artwork and the smell of gardenias. Odell might be right about one thing. The elderly woman living in the tower did appear to be in her own world. What had she done with the painting she'd taken? Probably put it up on a wall. At least no one would see it.

Pulling the newspaper from under her shirt, she dropped it and the rest of the paper on the table before glancing out the window. She caught a glimpse of Alma Garcia standing at her window overlooking the courtyard. Had she been listening to the conversation about ghosts? Apparently she had since she looked upset.

Willa followed the older woman's gaze. Alma seemed to be glaring down not at Odell and Henri who were talking by the pool but at Blossom, who was partially hidden from view where she stood in the shade along the back wall of the villa.

The girl looked as if she was eavesdropping on Odell's and Henri's conversation. Blossom looked up. Her piercing gaze seemed to meet Willa's, almost daring her.

Willa dropped the blind back into place and picked up the newspaper article she'd taken from Odell's room and turned it over.

All the breath rushed out of her. Earlier she'd been so shocked to see her own photo in the paper that she hadn't even noticed a second story—and photograph.

This one was of a younger Landry Jones.

He was wearing a police uniform!

Dropping in a chair, her gaze flew to the headline. Undercover Officer Wanted For Murder Of Partner: Manhunt Continues For Killer Cop—And Only Witness.

Willa quickly read the newspaper articles. The story had been broken by the news media after discovering that the police were involved in an intense but secret manhunt for plainclothes detective Landry Jones of the St. Petersburg Police Department.

Jones was wanted for the murder of his partner, Zeke Hartung after an eyewitness saw Jones kill Hartung outside a St. Pete Beach art gallery.

The police commissioner refused to discuss rumors that the two had been working undercover at the time of the murder or had turned on each other after infiltrating a criminal organization.

An inside source not to be named by the paper said Landry Jones had been working for known crime boss Freddy Delgado and had been hired for the contracted killings of Zeke Hartung and another undercover police officer, Simon Renton. Simon Renton's mutilated body had been found at a favorite organized-crime dumping site the day after Zeke Hartung's murder.

An inside news source said Renton's body had been identified by a tattoo on the torso because it had been impossible to get prints from the badly mutilated body.

Willa felt sick. No wonder the police had insisted on putting her in protective custody. Unfortunately they'd failed to tell her anything about Landry Jones. Or what he was involved in. Organized crime. Contract killings of two police officers.

She looked at Landry Jones's photo. The caption under it read Dirty Cop? Landry Jones Wanted For Questioning In The Brutal Murders Of Two Other Officers.

As she turned the page to finish the story, her gaze fell on a third photograph.

Willa gasped. It was the same man who'd come into her art studio the night before her gallery show.

The caption under the photograph read Undercover Cop Simon Renton Found Dead.

Willa was shaking so hard she had to put down the newspaper. Simon Renton was the man who had come into her studio the night she was finishing the last of the framing for her gallery show the next night. Now he was dead? Murdered? She shuddered. His body mutilated.

She dropped the newspaper. Simon and Landry were both cops, both working undercover on the same case. An icy chill wrapped around her neck. One man had come into her shop saying he needed a painting for his wife for their anniversary. The other had come to her gallery showing saying he was interested in the artist and her work.

Her pulse jumped. Both had lied. According to the story, Simon wasn't married. And a man like Landry wasn't interested in Willa's art—or her.

What had Simon Renton being doing in her shop that night? She shivered, remembering how he'd almost pushed his way in. He'd made her uncomfortable although she had the feeling he'd been trying to do just the opposite.

Something connected her with the two men. But she had no idea what. Both men had supposedly taken an interest in her artwork and now she was running for her life.

Not just from the police who were apparently doing their best to protect her, but from Landry Jones and organized criminals who it seemed might have a reason also to want her dead. It made no sense.

According to the paper, the safe house had been attacked by two known organized-crime hit men, the article said. Percy "TNT" Armando and Emilio "Worm" Racini. Both were being sought by the police after appearing on media cameras at the scene.

Was it possible that no one had seen Landry Jones but her? She'd just assumed he'd killed her two guards. If not, then what was he doing at the safe house?

Chasing her, she thought with a shudder. Making sure his buddies got the job done.

She had to get out off the island. She didn't know where she'd go—just that she had to keep moving. She'd been a fool to think she could hide out—even here—for a few weeks until Landry was caught.

But she'd run out of highway. Out of luck, as well. Landry could find her here. He was a cop, a renegade cop, but still he was trained for this. He had resources that ordinary people like herself didn't have. And he had organized crime behind him. She didn't stand a chance.

She wanted to curl up in a ball. Hastily she wiped at her tears. She didn't have the time to break down let alone feel sorry for herself. And giving up wasn't an option. She would go across the island to where Odell said the old man fished in his boat.

She'd ask him to take her back to the mainland. If he agreed, she'd come back and pack.

Now that her picture was in the paper, she wouldn't feel safe anywhere.

Just the thought of Landry Jones sent a chill through her. Look how close he'd come to getting to her at the safe house. She could still remember the murderous look in his eyes. She felt another wave of hopelessness. If she had any hope of surviving, she had to be strong. She'd stayed alive this long, hadn't she?

At the window, she peeked out. The courtyard was empty. Odell's door was closed. Willa let the blind fall back into place and opened her door, listening for a moment before she started down the stairs.

She heard music, this time coming from Blossom's apartment. Some awful loud band yelling obscenities over the scream of guitar strings.

Willa took the stairs, stopping partway to check to see if Henri's door was closed. It was.

Something told Willa that Henri wasn't in her apartment—not with that horrible music blasting into her south side wall.

As Willa hurried out of the courtyard through the back arch, she caught a glimpse of Henri and Odell walking down the beach. They had their heads together as if they'd known each other longer than less than an hour.

The conversation looked pretty serious for two strangers.

Willa put the two of them out of her mind. Soon they wouldn't be a concern. Soon, she would be off the island. She would go to Miami, maybe catch a boat to anywhere it was headed, anywhere far from here.

She found a narrow path through the thick vegetation, hoping this was the way that the elderly man had gone and that the path would lead her to the boathouse and Carlos Lazarro.

Not far into the dense undergrowth the air became thick and humid. Mosquitoes buzzed around her. She swatted at them and tried to keep moving, her bare limbs glistening with perspiration.

At a turn in the trail, she stopped to wipe the sweat from her eyes and thought she heard a sound behind her on the trail. Quickening her pace, she wound through the trees and brush, the island becoming denser. She felt turned around, no longer able to see the sun, and had no idea which way she was headed. For all she knew she could be going in a circle. The island wasn't large. She should have reached the other side by now.

Willa stopped to catch her breath. The trail forked ahead and she wasn't sure which way to go. This time there was no mistake about it. She heard the brush of fabric against a tree branch. Someone was following her.

Fear paralyzed her. She looked back but could see nothing through the underbrush. After reading the newspaper articles she now knew that it wasn't just the cops and Landry Jones after her—but possibly organized crime killers who didn't want her testifying.

She started down one path, afraid she was only getting farther and farther away from the villa—and more and more in danger. A twig cracked not far down the trail behind her.

A soft pop was instantly followed by leaves and bark flying up on a tree trunk next to her. Another soft pop, then a limb next to her exploded.

Someone was shooting at her!

Run!

She took off, running as fast and hard as she could, running blindly as the path twisted and turned. She could hear footfalls behind her, then another pop as a bullet buzzed past her ear and ripped through the leaves of a bush ahead of her.

She stumbled and just as she thought she might go down was grabbed from behind. An arm came around her, picking her up off her feet as a hand covered her mouth. She was jerked backward into the bushes and trees, her body slamming into the solid form of a man's chest as he tightened his grip.

"Don't make a sound or you're as good as dead." Her blood froze as she recognized the male voice that whispered at her ear as she was dragged backward into the darkness of the dense tropical forest.

Landry Jones.

Hadn't she known it was only a matter of time before he found her?

Chapter Eight

Landry dragged a struggling Willa St. Clair deep into the trees. She tried to bite his hand, connected several good kicks to his shins and jabbed him in the ribs with her elbow. Pain rocketed through him as she hit too close to his bandaged gunshot wound.

Angrily he tightened his grip on her and pressed his lips close to her ear. “Do that again and I will kill you myself right here.”

Keeping his hand firmly over her mouth, he dragged her a little deeper into the dense undergrowth and threw her down, pinning her to the ground as he sprawled on top of her and drew his gun with his free hand.

Her eyes blazed with anger and stark terror. Even against the odds and his threats, she still struggled to free herself. The woman was a scrapper. Under other circumstances he might have admired that.

He leaned close. “Quiet,” he whispered, and pressed his body down over hers as he listened. He thought he heard someone moving along the path not far from them. He held his breath, knowing how vulnerable he was in this position. All he could hope was that whoever was on the path didn't spot them. He wasn't sure he could get in a shot before someone else did.

Minutes passed. Finally he heard footfalls retreat back down the path. He waited until he was sure the person was gone before he holstered his gun and pulled Willa St. Clair to her feet. Still keeping her mouth covered, he dragged her back through the trees.

On this side of the island, the surf from the Gulf broke over the rocky shoreline. It was loud enough, it would muffle any sounds that she made. He dragged her to a short stretch of sandy beach where he'd pulled up the borrowed boat he'd hidden in the brush.

Tossing his weapon onto the duffel bag lying in the bottom of his boat, he dragged her out into the water until they were waist-deep.

"Now listen to me," he said next to her ear. "I'm going to remove my hand from your mouth. You're going to be smart and not scream or fight me. And then we're going to talk. Got it?"

Her body was still rigid with stubborn determination. But she nodded and he removed his hand, knowing without a doubt what she would do.

She took a swing at him and opened her mouth to scream.

He ducked the swing, grabbed her and hurled her into the deeper water, forcing her head under before she could get out a sound. He held her there, his hand tangled in her short curly dark hair, until some of the fight went out of her, then he dragged her to the surface.

She came up spitting and sputtering, murder in her eyes.

"What part of that didn't you get?" he demanded as he dunked her under again.

She gulped for air as he brought her up choking on the saltwater, but at the same time glaring at him. He watched her eyes and saw what she planned to do before she tried to scratch his eyes out.

He shoved her head under water again, holding her down longer this time, half-afraid he'd drown her before she'd give up. He jerked her to the surface and felt some of the fight go out of her.

"Why don't you just kill me and get it over with," she cried, choking and coughing as she came up. "First you shoot at me, then try to drown me?"

He shook his head. "I hit what I shoot at. If I wanted you dead, you'd already be dead. I saved your puny butt back there on the trail."

She gave a chortle of disbelief.

"Look, sweetheart, I could have broken your neck back there off the trail," he said, getting angry. "Or I could drown you right now. I'm not trying to kill you. I'm just trying to get you to quit fighting me. The last thing I want is you dead."

Willa stared at him, hating him. He'd turned her life upside down. How had she ever thought he was handsome? He was cruel and horrible. She glared at him, wanting to hit him but he held her at arm's length, his fingers tangled in her hair, and she knew if she tried, he would just dunk her again. Her eyes burned from the saltwater—and anger.

"If I let go of you, are you going to attack me again? Scream? Try to get away?"

She narrowed her eyes at him. "Would it do me any good?"

"None. All you'd accomplish is making sure whoever was shooting at you knows where we are and get us both killed."

He let go of her hair and stepped toward the beach, extending his hand as if to help her ashore.

She took a step back, the water up to her breasts now.

"Look, I'm not going to hurt you, okay?"

"Isn't that what all killers say? You probably told your partner that before you shot him."

A flicker of pain crossed Landry Jones's face and she thought for a moment he *would* drown her. He looked like he wanted to. Instead, he turned and waded through the water up to the beach. Stopping, he turned to look at her.

"See?" he said, holding out his hands. "And for the record, Zeke tried to kill *me*. It was self-defense."

She eyed him suspiciously. "If that were true, then why are the police looking for you?"

He sighed heavily. "It's my word against yours. All you saw was me shoot him. You obviously didn't see him try to kill me."

"Right. That's probably why the police didn't find a gun on him."

Landry made a low animal-like sound. "I saw you panic and take off. I came after you. Obviously someone took Zeke's gun to make me look guilty."

"Obviously."

He shook his head. "I don't care what you believe, all right? Now come out of the water. I already told you I'm not going to hurt you."

A wave slapped her in the back, throwing her forward. She took a few steps toward him and stopped. He retreated even farther up the beach to give her space.

Don't trust this guy. Do not—repeat—trust this guy.

"You still think I was the one shooting at you back there?" He walked over to where he'd tossed his weapon before dragging her into the Gulf, picked it up and held the gun out for her to look at it. "You see a silencer on here?"

She stared at the revolver in his hand. No silencer. The person shooting at her on the path had a silencer on his gun. She felt her body go limp with the realization that more than one person on this island wanted her dead.

"You are smart enough to know the sound a gun makes without one, aren't you?" he asked sarcastically.

"How do I know you didn't take off the silencer before you grabbed me?"

He rolled his eyes. "Why would I do that?"

She didn't know. In fact, all she knew about this man was that she'd seen him shoot his partner, that apparently before that he'd been a police officer, and that he was now wanted by the law. The fact that she was the only witness to that shooting put her in a precarious position to say the least.

"I have no reason to trust anything you say."

He stared at her as if she'd just said something astounding, then he groaned, pulled off the cap he'd been wearing and raked a hand through his full head of dark hair. "What am I going to do with you?"

"I was wondering the same thing."

"Sweetheart, do you have any idea how many people want you dead? There are people waiting in *line* to kill you."

"Don't call me sweetheart," she snapped back.

"What I'm trying to tell you is that there is a massive manhunt going on for you right now."

She lifted a brow. "For you, as well, it seems."

He smiled. And for just an instant she forgot that she didn't find him handsome. "Point taken."

He reached into the shorts pocket, drew out a wet crumpled photograph and held it out. Reluctantly she stepped close and took it, recognizing the man in the picture at once.

"You remember him." It wasn't a question. He'd seen her reaction to Simon Renton's photograph. "He came into your art studio the night before your gallery showing. He left something there. I need it back."

So that was why she was still alive. He needed something from her. "And you think I have it?"

"I *know* you have it. Or at least can help me find it and end all of this."

And she had a pretty good idea just how it would end.

She glanced down the beach. The tide was coming in. The surf pounded at the rocks off to her left. To her right the short sandy beach ended in a throng of mangroves. Her only chance was getting past Landry and making a run for it back up the trail.

But even if she managed to get past him, she knew she wouldn't get far back in the brush and trees. And taking off swimming would be suicide even if he didn't come after her and drown her. Not to mention, the person who'd been shooting at her could be waiting in the trees.

"Look, I know what you're thinking," he said, his voice softening. "But you're out of places to run. There's already someone on the island taking potshots at you. It's just a matter of time before they kill you."

This, at least, sounded true. She said nothing, just looked at him, wondering what it was he thought she had and what possible chance she had of surviving this.

"You have a problem?" he asked.

She glared at him, realizing she was beyond caring right now if he shot her or drowned her or broke her neck. "Kind of the same one. I don't believe anything you tell me."

"You have quite the mouth on you, Ms. Willa St. Clair." He took a step toward her, backing her to the edge of the water, his gaze locked on her lips. "Quite a nice mouth, actually."

She felt herself squirm under the heat of those dark eyes. She was at his mercy, completely alone with a man she knew was a killer. But she also sensed that backing down would only make her more vulnerable—if that were possible. She stood her ground as he stepped so close that she could see tiny gold flecks in that dark gaze and feel heat radiating from his body.

"If you expect me to help you, then I suggest you stop threatening me," she said, surprised her voice could sound so calm with her pulse thundering in her ears. "All you're doing is convincing me you're exactly the man I think you are and certainly not one to be trusted."

His hand came up so quickly it took everything in her not to flinch. His fingertips were cool and rough as they trailed across her cheek to her lips. He dragged one finger over her lower lip, his gaze never leaving her eyes, then trailed it down her throat, stopping at her collarbone.

She held her breath and wondered just how far Landry Jones would go to get whatever it was he thought she had.

He drew back his fingertips and stepped away.

She let herself take a breath, her body trembling, suddenly more afraid than when he'd held her under water. There were worse things than death.

LANDRY WAS LOSING patience—with this woman—and with himself. He was used to getting what he wanted. Even Freddy D.'s men knew better than to push him too far.

For most of the past two years, he'd worked undercover, using intimidation like a weapon. Maybe he'd been undercover and around men like Freddy D. for too long.

But this woman was also exasperating as all hell. She was nothing like the mild-mannered Willa St. Clair he'd asked out for coffee the night of her art showing. Funny how just a few days could change a person. Or had all this steel been under all that sweet innocence?

Well, if she'd changed, he had only himself to blame for it. Seeing a man shot down in front of her had to have an effect. Especially on a woman like Willa St. Clair. He'd had a friend of his on the force do some checking on the artist. He suspected she was as squeaky-clean and green behind the ears as she seemed to be.

Or had been. Now she was on the run and desperate. He knew from experience that that alone could change a person.

He raked a hand through his hair and sighed. "Let me lay it out for you. I infiltrated a crime organization operating out of southern Florida. After a while Zeke came in and then Simon." He looked past her to the gulf, his eyes dark. "We worked for a man named Freddy D."

"Freddy Delgado," she said.

He nodded, wondering if she knew more than he did at this point. Was it possible she'd already found the disk?

"We knew Freddy had a cop in his pocket," he continued, watching her face for any sign that she was way ahead of him. "My job was to find the dirty cop." He touched his tongue to his lower lip, eyes darkening. Her expression hadn't changed. "I had several leads on cops who Freddy was paying off to look the other way, but they were small potatoes. The guy I was looking for would have to be close to Freddy. Real close. As it turns out, real close to me, as well."

"You're telling me Zeke was the dirty cop." She didn't sound like she believed it for a minute. "But you said he came into the organization undercover *after* you."

He smiled. The woman was sharp. And she'd been paying attention. "Yeah, so now you understand why I was blindsided. I never suspected Zeke. Why would I?"

Her hair was wet. It curled around her lightly freckled face. Her eyes were wide and blue. She couldn't have looked more adorable—even with the straight blond hair she'd had the night he met her. It hit him that under other circumstances, he really would have asked her out that night after the art show. She had that much of an impact on him.

"Give me one good reason to believe anything you're telling me is the truth," she said, those big blues narrowing.

He studied her for a moment, then lifted his shirt to show her the wound in his side. "When Zeke walked up to the car that night, I didn't see the gun in his hand until it was almost too late."

She flinched at the sight of his wound. "How do I know you didn't get shot when you attacked the safe house where the police were keeping me?"

He raised his hands slowly as if in surrender. "What is it going to take to get through to you? Isn't it possible I was trying to save you?"

Her gaze said, *Not a chance in hell.*

THE GUNSHOT WOUND HAD surprised her. She could see where he'd been shot. The area was red and angry, although clearly starting to heal. *Someone* had shot him. Was it possible Zeke's had been one of the shots she'd heard that night?

She thought of Simon Renton, remembering how he'd lied about wanting a painting for his anniversary, a painting his wife had picked out. She'd foolishly opened the door and let him in that night even though every instinct warned her not to.

"What did Simon leave in my studio?" she asked as she realized her only hope was to find out what was going on, what Landry Jones wanted from her.

He seemed to relax a little. "A disk. Simon put it between a painting and the backing." Landry's gaze softened. "You saved him and the disk that night."

"At what cost to my own life since he still died?" she said angrily. "And for what? Some stupid disk?" She shuddered. "Do you think it was worth it for him to be tortured to death? He still told them about the disk and the painting, didn't he?"

Landry looked away. "Simon knew what was at stake. We were all risking our lives to bring down an organization that steals, kills and pollutes all of our lives."

She said nothing, not sure what to believe. "What's on this disk?"

"If I told you that, I would have to kill you."

She looked at him, narrowing her eyes. "You think that's funny?"

"Actually, truthful. I'm serious, Willa. That's why I have to find that disk before Freddy D. and his men do."

It was the first time he'd called her Willa. She hated that he used her name in that soft tone of his and it had an effect on her.

"Aren't the police looking for it, too?" she asked, and saw the answer in his expression. "You want to find it before the police do, and you tell me you have nothing to hide?"

"It's complicated. The bottom line is that the disk is worth killing—or dying—for. You're going to help me find it. One way or the other."

"Back to threats? What will you do to me? Try to drown me again? Torture me? Beat me up?"

He groaned. "What do you want?"

"How about the truth? What's on the disk?"

"Important information about organized crime in southern Florida—names, numbers, enough to shut down these people."

She waited, staring at him.

He groaned again. "There's also proof on the disk that I didn't kill Zeke in cold blood. Proof that it was self-defense because the name of the dirty cop is on that disk. That disk will clear me."

"Or condemn you," she said.

He smiled and settled his gaze on her. "Either way, I need the disk. I'm asking you to trust me and help me find it."

Trust him? How could she, given what she knew? "How do I know that once you have the disk you won't kill me?" She couldn't suppress a grimace.

He raised a brow. "You don't. But without me, sweetheart, you're dead. Someone on this island obviously knows who you are and has been paid to come here and kill you." He smiled. "You left a trail anyone could follow. You think they're going to let you off this island alive without my help?"

He had a point. He'd found her and obviously someone else had. Unless, of course, he was the one who'd shot at her. But would he take such a chance when he needed her alive to help him find the disk?

The alternative was that he was right. Someone on the island wanted her dead. Other than Landry Jones.

"We need each other," he said.

"At least until you find the disk."

He shook his head in obvious frustration. "You want to get off this island alive? Help me and I'll help you. Maybe by the time we find the disk, you'll realize you can trust me."

Maybe. But she doubted it. Even if Landry Jones wasn't a murderer, he was dangerous. Especially to a small-town girl from South Dakota.

She looked toward the trail and again thought about trying to make a break for it. If she could reach Carlos, get him to take her to the mainland…

As she started past Landry, he grabbed her wrist so quickly she hadn't even seen the movement. His fingers clamped down. "Don't underestimate me, though. That would be a mistake."

She winced in pain and he loosened his grip, turning her hand over and opening his fingers. He frowned down at the bruises on her wrist.

"Who did this?" he asked, sounding angry.

This from a man who had just held her under the water. "I almost fell in the pool last night at the villa. One of the residents grabbed me." She rubbed at her wrist as she pulled it free.

"One of the residents?" he repeated. "You sure he was trying to save you?"

She wasn't sure of anything, and it must have showed. "How did you know it was a he?"

Landry only smiled. "I think you'd better tell me about the other people on the island before we go back."

"We're going back to the villa?" she asked in surprise. She'd figured they would be going back to the mainland. And she would get away from him.

"Don't you think it would be wise to find out who on this island might have reason to want you dead?" he asked.

"You mean other than you." Her sarcasm wasn't wasted on him.

"I'm amazed you've stayed alive this long," he said, stepping past her to pick up his backpack.

Now that she knew what was at stake, Willa was surprised herself. But as she looked into Landry's handsome face she was reminded again that there were worse things than death. Taking him back to the villa with her could be one of them.

"And how exactly do you intend to explain your appearance on the island?" she asked. "All the apartments are full."

"You let me worry about that," he said. "Tell me about everyone on the island."

Willa told him about Odell, Henri and Blossom. Landry listened, and when she finished she had the strangest feeling that he'd already known all of it.

She recalled the animal-like movement she'd seen from the balcony last night. It hadn't been Odell. It had been Landry. She was sure of it. "How long have you been on the island?" she demanded.

Landry grinned. "Long enough to know what you sleep in."

She felt her face heat as she remembered her little foray behind the villa with the shovel. "You were spying on me last night?"

"Look, the tide is coming in. We're losing our beach. Pretty soon we'll be arguing about this underwater." He turned his back on her and started through the trees.

She didn't move even when she felt a wave wash around her ankles.

He disappeared into the trees and she was considering taking the boat and making a run for it, when he returned looking irritable at best.

"What?" he asked, hands on his hips.

"Did you see what happened by the pool last night?" she asked.

He shook his head. "I came running when I heard you scream but by then your friend Odell had already saved you."

"He isn't my friend," she snapped. She was angry at Landry for spying on her. But even more angry that he hadn't seen what had happened before Odell showed up at the pool. "So are you going to tell me which painting Simon hid the disk in?"

"No." He started to turn toward the trees again but must have seen that she wasn't moving an inch until he told her. "It's a painting of a sailboat. That's all you need to know right now."

A painting of sailboat? She had done dozens of those.

"You're just going to have to trust me."

She stared at him. Trust him? He had to be kidding. Did she even believe him? She believed he was after something. Possibly *that* was the only reason she was still alive. What she feared was that there was something on the disk that Landry Jones needed to save himself, all right. He needed the disk so he could destroy it for his boss Freddy D.—and save the truth from coming out about him. And once she was dead there wouldn't be anyone to testify against him. It would be his word against a dead man's.

He smiled. "Calculating the odds?" His question took her by surprise.

"What odds?"

"Whether I'm lying to you or not."

He'd hit too close to home and she knew it must have shown in her expression. "Just my luck that Simon picked *your* art studio."

"My thoughts exactly."

He shook his head and settled his gaze on her. "Look, if all I wanted was the disk, wouldn't I just kill you and go through your stuff? Apparently that's what the person who was shooting at you had planned." He raised a brow in question.

"And they would have been very disappointed," she said. "I don't have any of my paintings with me."

That got his attention. "Where are they?"

She just looked at him and said nothing.

His jaw muscle jumped, his eyes darkened.

Clearly they had reached a stalemate. It was her turn to smile. "Who doesn't trust whom?"

"You're starting to burn," he said, and cocked his head toward the sun beating down on them. "We need to get you back to the villa." But he didn't move. "Don't you want to hear my plan?"

From his pleased expression? No. "What?" Her voice

cracked. She had a bad feeling she knew exactly what he was about to suggest.

"The way I see it, someone on this island knows who you are. They could be searching your apartment right now. Or maybe planning to wait until tonight to break in, kill you and search it."

"That's crazy," she said, but rubbed her wrist, remembering last night by the pool and the gunshots only minutes before.

"Is it crazy? If those bullets would have found their mark earlier, you'd be shark bait." He must have seen her surprise. "You think your body would ever be found?" He chuckled. "As far as everyone is concerned, you've disappeared. So the simplest thing is for your body to end up as fish food. No one would ever have to know what happened to you." He sounded as if he'd given this some thought. "You're in over your head, sweetheart. You've got one chance and that's me." He grinned wickedly at her.

She didn't like his smugness. Nor was she sure Landry Jones's help was what she needed at all. She dug her heels in, even though the water was now washing around her thighs. "It sounds to me like you need *mine* since I'm the only one who knows where the painting is."

"So we work together."

There was no doubt in her mind that once he had the disk he would be long gone. "What's in it for me?" she asked.

He blinked in surprise. "Excuse me? When I have the

disk, I clear my name and put some major scumbags in prison. You, sweetheart, get to keep breathing."

"I told you not to call me sweetheart." She felt his gaze go to the front of her wet T-shirt. More specifically to her breasts poking against the thin fabric of her bra and the wet fabric.

She crossed her arms over her chest and he had the good grace to look sheepish as he raised his eyes to her face again.

"I'm sorry. What did you say?" he asked, eyes hooded.

She glared at him, knowing darn well he'd heard her.

"So where are your paintings?" he asked.

She gave him a like-I'm-just-going-to-tell-you look.

"Fine. Want to take your chances without me, sweetheart? Up to you. I'll track down your paintings without you since I'm betting you'll be swimming with the sharks by midnight."

"Stop calling me sweetheart and I'll consider your offer."

He raised a brow. "My offer?"

It was simple enough. Even if he was lying, he would keep her alive until they found the disk. If he was telling the truth, once she knew which painting Simon Renton had hid the disk in all she had to do was find it first and get it to the police....

His gaze lazily caressed her face, a grin tugging at his lips. He had a pretty great mouth on him, too, she noticed. "First, let's discuss my cover. I'm your boyfriend."

"No way."

He didn't seem to hear her. "I got a ride out to the island to meet you here." He reached into the boat and brought out a duffel bag reminding her of Blossom's duffel. "We're lovers just having a nice vacation."

His grin made her stomach flip-flop. "I told you the painting isn't on the island."

"I'd like to make sure myself. I'm from Missouri, you know, the Show Me State?"

So that's why they were going back to the villa. "Whatever. Don't believe me. What about the person who wants me dead?"

"I'll take care of that, as well."

She eyed him. "Like you did Zeke?" She saw at once that she'd hit a sore spot.

"Zeke was my friend. I don't know what the hell happened, what made him do what he did." Landry's eyes darkened. "But do me a favor, don't bring him up unless you want to make me mad, okay, sweet—" He caught himself. "Okay?"

She nodded.

They stood glaring at each other for a long moment, the water rising around them. Then he said, "Can we go meet your island mates now, darlin'?" Before she could protest, he added, "I can't call you Willa. I have to call you something and we *are* lovers." That wicked grin again.

She wanted to wipe it off his face. But instead, she stalked past him. He grabbed her arm and spun her around to face him.

"You should let me go first. Just in case we run into one of your neighbors, the one with the gun," he said with a lift of his brow. "If that's all right with you, darlin'."

Chapter Nine

Willa groaned as she stared at his arrogant backside. She was sure she heard him chuckle and hated him all the more as she followed him through the trees and underbrush.

It was cool in the trees. She felt flushed. From the sun. From being around this impossible man. But if this stupid disk would get her life back, she would find it. What choice did she have but let Landry Jones accompany her? He knew which painting the disk was hidden in. She didn't. At least not yet.

The quiet in the trees unnerved her. Was the person who'd shot at her waiting nearby, planning to finish the job this time? More to the point, would Landry Jones save her again?

"Are you really?" she asked as she quickened her step so she was right behind his broad back.

"Am I really what?"

"From Missouri?"

He glanced over his shoulder at her. “Yeah.” A bird squawked off to their right, making them both jump. “Gotta ask you, why’d you pick this island of all the damned islands? Ten Thousand Islands and you pick this one.”

“What’s wrong with it?”

“Are you serious? Can’t you feel it? The place gives me the creeps. What horrible thing *hasn’t* happened here? Only you would pick a haunted damned island to hide out on.”

“You don’t really believe the island is haunted,” she said, scoffing at such foolishness.

He glanced around uneasily. “Bad things have happened here, darlin’. Maybe you can’t sense it, but I can. And you know what they say about places like this….”

“No,” she said, telling herself he was just trying to scare her. “What do they say?”

“Bad things will happen again. Evil attracts evil. It’s a known fact.”

He wasn’t serious. The next thing she knew he’d be out burying a jar behind the villa. “You’re a strange guy, Landry.”

He turned to look at her and grinned. “You don’t know the half of it.”

And that’s what worried her.

LANDRY SLOWED at they reached the rear of the villa. He could hear voices and music playing. His stomach growled as he caught the scent of barbecue.

"Looks like we made it back just in time," he said over his shoulder.

Odell looked up in surprise as Landry came through the archway into the courtyard. Odell and Henri were sitting together in a pair of old metal lawn chairs outside his apartment. There was a bottle of wine on a small table between them, two mismatched plastic glasses and a deck of cards.

"Nice pool," Landry whispered to Willa.

Her gaze went to the dark water, then Odell. He had turned and was watching them with interest. Too much interest.

Clearly the two of them had interrupted something because Henri looked surprised to see them and maybe a little suspicious. Landry had seen the redhead and the devil child arrive this morning by boat. Thanks to Willa, he now had their names. If only he could have easily found out what they were doing on the island.

But he was more interested in Odell. Everything about the man worried him. Especially Odell's obvious interest in Willa.

"I made it," Landry said cheerfully, and put his arm around Willa, pulling her close. She nudged him.

"Look who surprised me," she said, as if trying to match his cheerfulness. She looked scared and war,y as well, of her villa mates.

"You go swimming?" Odell asked, lifting a brow as he took in their wet clothing.

Landry grinned and pulled Willa closer. "I was so

glad to see her I didn't even give her a chance to take off her clothes." He chuckled and let his gaze move appreciatively over her. That at least he didn't have to pretend. She had a great body and wet clothing left nothing to the imagination. "We really should get out of these clothes, darlin'."

Henri laughed. "My kind of man."

Odell turned his attention back to the redhead.

As Landry led Willa past the two, he saw that they had been playing poker. Strip poker from the little they were both wearing—and the pile of clothing beside the table.

Odell was down to his shorts. Henri was wearing a string bikini.

As Willa and Landry passed them, Landry took a good look at the full swell of Henri's breasts in the tiny bikini top.

Willa elbowed him even harder this time and smiled as he rewarded her with a satisfyingly painful grunt. She slipped out from under his arm and ran up the stairs ahead of him. At the top, she turned to look back and caught him admiring her butt. She glared at him.

He shook his head and laughed as he charged up the stairs and pinned her against the wall, leaning down to kiss her neck and whisper, "You can't have it both ways, darlin'."

"Well, we know what those two are going to be doing the rest of the day," Henri said, loud enough for them to hear.

"You should change and join us," Odell said. "Don't worry, I have enough steaks for everyone."

Landry didn't like what he heard in the man's invitation. Odell sounded upset. Because he was jealous? Or because the last thing Odell wanted was anyone in Willa's room tonight?

WILLA WAS TRYING desperately to ignore Landry. It was more than difficult given that he was nibbling on her neck and sending tingles through her body. She tried to shove him away, but he was much stronger and he seemed to be enjoying what he was doing. Unfortunately her body was reacting. She felt her nipples harden.

Landry pulled back to look down at her chest then grinned as he met her eyes. "Glad to see you're getting into your role."

She would have hit him if he hadn't had her pinned against the wall with his body. "You really are despicable," she hissed so only he could hear.

His grin broadened. He bent again to tease her throat with kisses and suddenly froze. She turned her head in the direction he was looking and saw Alma Garcia. The woman stood as if poleaxed, staring in horror at Landry just feet from them.

She said something in Spanish, then quickly crossed herself.

Willa gripped Landry's arm, frightened by the crazed look in the older woman's eyes. Willa could feel Odell and Henri watching the scene from below, as if spellbound.

Landry said something to Alma also in Spanish. The woman drew back, her hand going to her throat, tears welling in her eyes and spilling down her cheeks. Then she turned and practically ran, her antique gown rustling as she disappeared through the arch at the end of the walk.

"What was *that* about?" Willa whispered on an expelled breath.

"Welcome to the looney bin," Odell called up.

"Wow, that was scary," Henri said. "What did she say to you?"

"Mistaken identity," Landry said with a laugh and drew Willa down the walkway to the door of the apartment, keeping his hand firmly on her arm.

She fumbled out the key and the moment the door opened, Landry pushed her inside and closed the door after them.

"What the hell was that?" he whispered, even though no one could hear them.

"You tell *me*."

He looked pale and she felt a tremor go through him as he held on to her arm.

"She called me her amour, her love, then asked me what I was doing back here. Did you see the look in her eyes?"

Willa nodded. "Don't ever do that again."

He stared at her. "What?"

"That," she snapped, pointing back toward the balcony.

His eyes narrowed. "I thought I made it clear. Whoever is trying to kill you needs to believe we're lovers."

"Bull. Wouldn't it be more effective to tell them you're my brother the cop? Or even better, the FBI?"

He smiled. "We should have thought of that before we told them we were lovers."

She daggered a look at him, wondering if she could hate him any more.

"That old woman—she lives here?" he asked, obviously more shaken by that than any look Willa could fire at him.

"Her name is Alma Garcia. She used to be the nanny here." Willa shivered from her wet clothing. She sighed and told him a shortened version of the story that Odell had told her. "I think Odell is writing a book about the disappearance of the family. But I also found a recent newspaper about…us. Complete with photos." She went to the table and picked up the newspaper and handed it to him, watching him as he stared at his photograph.

"How'd you get this?"

She squirmed a little. "I took it from Odell's room."

Landry looked up at her. "He's going to realize it's missing."

She shook her head. "He offered me the rest of the newspaper. So I took it. I'm just afraid he recognized me."

"Neither of us looks like this now," he said.

Landry was right. With his hair much longer and the designer stubble that was starting to be a close-cropped beard, he looked nothing like the clean-cut, clean-shaven cop in the photo. Now he looked more like a beach bum.

Or a pirate.

Is that why Alma thought she knew him? Hadn't Odell said that Alma's boss, Andres Santiago, was a modern-day pirate? Then others like him would have visited the island and apparently Alma had fallen for one of them. Fallen hard, given the way she'd looked at Landry with both love—and fear.

But why fear? Did she think that her pirate had caused the deaths of Andres and Medina and their children? Did she live in fear that the killer would come back for her, as well?

Or had Alma been afraid because as delusional as she might be, she'd seen a killer when she looked at Landry?

Willa felt a chill as she met his eyes.

"You should get a shower and change."

She shook her head and crossed her arms over her chest again. "You're going to tell me what painting we're looking for first."

Landry studied her, wondering what went on in that head of hers, suspecting he knew. "It's a blue sailboat bent in the wind with a red and white sail, small." He held his hands about eight inches apart, all the time watching her face. "It was marked for the art show but it wasn't there."

Her smile could have cut glass. "That's why you came to my show. You were only after the painting. Until you couldn't find it. Then you were after me." She looked like she might want to scratch his eyes out. "Just tell me this. What would have happened if Zeke hadn't come along when he did? If I would have gotten into your car with you?"

He didn't answer her. Instead, he glanced toward the bedroom. He could see her bed, a double all made up with pretty floral yellow-and-white sheets and a brightly colored spread of primary colors. It looked more than a little inviting since he hadn't had but a few fitful hours of sleep for the past seventy-two hours.

But unfortunately sleep was the last thing he thought of when he looked at Willa St. Clair's bed—and that made that bed damned dangerous.

Dragging his gaze away, he saw her easel, a painting on it. He stepped into the second room, glanced into the bathroom, then studied her artwork.

The painting was of the villa but there was something about it that made his stomach knot. One wall was blood-red. At first he thought it was bougainvillea, but on closer inspection it appeared to be splattered with blood as if a massacre had happened here.

He heard her step into the room, could feel her watching him. The painting was haunting. He pulled his gaze away to look at her, surprised by the effect of her painting on him, but maybe even more surprised by her talent and the effect *she had* on him.

"Well?"

He frowned, having forgotten the question.

"What did you plan to do to me the night of the art show?" she demanded, meeting his hooded gaze with a furious one of her own.

"You know the answer," he said, waving it off. "I needed the disk." He hated the hurt he saw in her expression. "Darlin', I'm a cop. I was doing my job, just like I'm doing right now, whether you believe me or not."

He looked at the painting again. It was like looking at a car wreck. You didn't want to look but you couldn't help yourself. "What the hell is this?" he asked, pointing at the red splatters on the wall.

She seemed to pull her gaze away from him, focusing slowly on the painting. "I don't know. It's just what I see. I paint what I see in my…mind."

He swore softly. "All your other stuff was nice sailboats, sunny days, warm turquoise water."

"That was before I witnessed a murder."

He sobered, softening as he looked at her. "I'm sorry you had to see that. Believe me it's given me a few nightmares, as well."

A silence fell between them. Willa felt herself softening toward Landry and mentally slapped herself.

"I know which painting you're talking about," she said after a moment. "But I don't know what happened to it."

"What?"

"I remember the painting. It was supposed to be in the show but I don't remember seeing it after the paintings went to the gallery."

He swore again. "Was it possible Simon hid the painting somewhere in your studio? The police searched the place, right?"

She nodded.

"Freddy D.'s not in jail so he knows the disk hasn't turned up. So where the hell was it?" She could hear his frustration and his fear. "Did anyone else have access to your shop?"

She shook her head. "Another artist who worked next door would sometimes watch the shop if I had to leave for a few minutes.... But she wasn't in the shop between when Simon Renton came in and I packed the items for the show."

"Okay, let's walk through what happened after Simon left your shop, okay?"

She explained how she had finished the last of the framing. "I was too excited to sleep so I packed up the art for the show, then I went to bed."

"And you're sure that painting was one of them you packed?"

She nodded.

"You say you went to bed?"

"My apartment was just upstairs."

"You think you would have heard if anyone had come in during the night?"

"Of course. Anyway, the paintings were packed. It would have been impossible for someone to sneak in, find that particular painting and take it without me hearing them."

He groaned and raked a hand through his hair. "Okay, the painting was packed, then what?"

"The next morning, Evan came over and helped me

load the paintings into a van and take them to the gallery. Evan is the gallery owner. I helped him put the boxes in the back of the shop. Then I left and he set up the show after the gallery closed that afternoon."

"He does everything himself?"

"It's a small gallery."

"What did you do?"

"I went back to my studio and worked. I like to paint when I'm anxious. It calms me. Later, I went over to the gallery to make sure Evan had everything he needed."

"But you don't remember seeing the sailboat painting."

"No, but then I can't be sure it wasn't there and disappeared later. Evan might remember."

Yes, Landry would have to talk to Evan. "Did all the paintings sell?"

"Almost all of them. Evan packed up the rest."

Landry felt his heart quicken. If the small painting had accidentally been overlooked in a box at the back of the gallery, Evan would have just packed the unsold ones with it. "What happened to those paintings, the unsold ones?"

She frowned. "I asked him to put them away for me until I came for them."

The painting had to be one of two places if it hadn't been found yet, which he was counting on. Either it had been misplaced at the gallery. Or Simon had hid it in the studio.

"Okay," he said, feeling better. "What happened to everything in your studio?"

"The police took me back there and I packed up everything."

"Did any of the officers help?" he asked.

"Two." She seemed to see where he was headed with this. "Yes, but no one walked away with a painting or a disk. They just made sure you didn't try to kill me while I told them what needed to be packed, and they did it. I watched the entire process."

He ignored the part about him killing her. As far as he knew, the police didn't know that Simon had hid the disk in a painting. Simon was dead so he couldn't have told them and Zeke wasn't about to tell them since he'd changed sides no doubt long before all of this had happened. So the police wouldn't be looking for the painting. That meant either of them could have unknowingly packed the painting with the disk, never suspecting what they had in their hands.

"Is it possible you missed the painting—it was small, so maybe you overlooked it and left it behind?" Especially if Simon had hidden it.

She shook her head. "I gave up the studio so everything was packed and cleaned out. There really wasn't anyplace to hide anything."

He nodded. "So where is everything you boxed up?"

"In storage."

He rolled his eyes. "I gathered that. Okay, darlin'," he said, his gaze locking with hers as he stepped toward her. "What do I have to do to get you to trust me?" he asked, his voice soft as he cupped her cheek.

She tried to step away from him, but he pressed her

to the wall with his body. She smelled clean and a little citrusy. He sniffed her hair, breathing her in.

Her big blue eyes were on him. He removed her glasses and tossed them aside; her eyes widened. He could feel her breath quicken. Her heart was a hammer in her chest. She really was something.

As he bent to kiss her, she tried to turn her head away but he was still cupping her cheek, still pinning her to the wall.

She glared at him as he lowered his mouth until his lips were only a hairbreadth above hers. He felt her breath catch as he lowered his mouth to hers.

He kissed her gently, slowly, carefully. At first it was to show her how things were going to be but somewhere along the way he felt things change. Not so much in her as in himself.

Her mouth was paradise. There was a shyness to her, an innocence he'd seen the first time he'd laid eyes on her and yet hadn't believed. It was still there though beneath the bravado. And he was surprisingly touched by it.

He drew back to look into her big blue eyes. She looked like a deer caught in headlights. Her tongue darted out to touch her lower lip. She looked scared and excited all at the same time. He could feel her heart pounding beneath his. Something had changed between them and he already regretted it.

Sometimes he hated his job, hated that he had to use people, to gain their trust, to hurt them.

He especially hated that in the end he would hurt Willa St. Clair.

WILLA LOOKED PAST him, her eyes growing wider. He swung around, going for his weapon, expecting to see someone behind them.

The room was empty. He blinked as he swung back around with the gun in his hand and faced her.

Willa stood smiling smugly. "I think we need to establish some ground rules," she said calmly, although he could see she was anything but.

"That was just a *ruse?*"

She cocked her head at him, still smiling. "Just like that kiss of yours was to make me think I could trust you."

He holstered his weapon, eyeing her warily. He understood now how she had managed to survive this long. And maybe the kiss had started out that way, but it had changed. He thought about calling her on it. She'd felt something. He knew because he'd felt it, too. But she was right about them needing some ground rules.

"Have you heard the story about the little boy who cried wolf?" he asked as he stepped closer.

"I like the one about the wolf in sheep's clothing better," she said, and held up her hand. "That's close enough. Rule number one: Keep your hands off me."

He grinned. "That won't be easy given that your neighbors think we're lovers and up here right now going at it on your bed."

She flushed and he had a flash of the two of them on the bed doing just that. He took a step back as he felt himself grow hard at the thought.

"What?" she asked, frowning.

He looked at her. Was she serious? "How many men have you been with?"

"What?"

He let out an oath and took another step back. "Don't tell me you're a virgin."

Landry looked horrified and Willa wanted to defend virgins all over the world. Instead, she kept her mouth shut, her face flushing and giving her away.

He let out another curse. "How old are you anyway?"

"Twenty-five, and you're wrong. I've been with plenty of men." She groaned inwardly. Why had she said that?

He started to laugh, shaking his head as he stared at her. "Twenty-five? Aren't there any able-bodied men in South Dakota?"

"No, there's only sheep," she snapped. "Of course there are men, and I told you, I've been with my share." Her chin went up.

"Then all the men are with the sheep," he said with a laugh.

"That isn't funny." Her voice broke.

He stopped laughing. "Sorry."

"Could we just concentrate on finding the painting and you stop ruining my life?"

He nodded solemnly. "I haven't ruined your life. At least I hope not." He took another step back.

"Would you stop treating me like I have some communicable disease?"

"Sorry. It's just that you're an attractive woman and I don't want to be the one who deflowers you."

She groaned. Deflower? Could she be any more mortified? "Don't worry about it. It's not like I would want you anyway."

"You're right. The first time should be with someone you love. Someone who respects you and wants your first time to be something wonderful."

"Could you please *stop?*" His words were getting to her. How could he sound so sensitive when she knew he was just the opposite? And he was still looking at her as if she was a freak of nature.

Was it possible that she could hate Landry Jones any more? Obviously it was. She glared at him, wanting to convince him he was wrong about her, but at the same time knowing she would be wasting her breath.

"The storage unit is in Everglades City," she burst out.

He blinked at her.

"Let's go," she said, and started for the door.

"Hold on," he said, grabbing her arm and then quickly letting go of it. "Sorry, forgot the ground rules," he said, acting as if she'd burned him.

She narrowed her gaze at him. It wasn't the ground rules that had made him behave the way he had. Men like Landry Jones didn't obey rules. The man was probably a killer, a dirty cop; he certainly was no gentleman. So why was he acting as if she had the plague because he thought she was a virgin? She'd bet he'd taken his share of virgins. So why draw the line with her? She felt insulted.

"We have to wait until everyone goes to bed around here," he said. "We can't just take off. Not unless we want to be followed by whoever tried to kill you earlier."

She hadn't thought of that. She'd been too angry with Landry. "Fine."

"In the meantime I think we should take Odell up on his offer of a steak."

"You have to be kidding." Having dinner with someone who wanted to kill her was the last thing on her mind.

"I would think a woman from South Dakota would eat beef."

She glared at him, still too angry with him to be civil. "Lamb and mutton, remember, all those sheep."

He laughed and glanced in her fridge. "Cottage cheese and fruit or yogurt." He closed the door. "Definitely think we should go to the barbecue."

"Fine." She didn't give him a chance to say anything as she stalked into the bedroom and started to close the door.

"No!" she cried. The next thing she knew Landry was at her side, his weapon in hand.

"Wait." Landry reached for her but she dodged his outstretched hand and rushed to her box of supplies.

"Oh, no," she said again as she dropped to her knees and began going through the box of supplies.

"What is it?" Landry asked after he quickly searched the bedroom and bathroom.

"Someone's gone through my things, only this time at least they didn't take my painting."

"Someone took a painting?" He sounded panicked.

From the floor, she looked up at him and mugged a face. "Not the painting you're interested in. This was one I did yesterday." Her eyes narrowed. "Did you take it?"

"No, why would I?" He looked insulted.

"Maybe it was Alma then. I smelled gardenias."

"Gardenias," he repeated, looking lost.

Nothing appeared to be missing this time, but someone had definitely gone through her stuff and she had to wonder who else had a key to her apartment. She felt violated, which seemed crazy since she was already running for her life and now living with a possible killer. What could be worse than that? Having someone paw through her private things.

"What was the painting?" Landry asked, hunching down on the floor next to her. He seemed concerned by how upset she was. Or maybe he was just worried that the same thief had his painting.

"It was—" she hesitated, remembering the painting "—of the murder in front of the gallery."

He winced. "Of me?"

She nodded, and he swore softly.

"Great," he said.

She glanced toward the painting on the easel, wondering why whoever had taken the other painting hadn't taken this one.

He shoved to his feet with a sigh. "Show me all of the paintings you have."

She looked up at him. "I told you the one you want isn't here."

"Or I can look myself," he said, his jaw muscle tightening.

She stood, copying his sigh. She crossed her arms. Her clothing had finally dried out some but she still felt half-naked around him. She couldn't help but think of the kiss, of what it felt like being in his arms, or the look on his face when she'd rushed from those arms and fooled him, she thought with a smile.

"What?"

She shook her head. "Go ahead. I know you aren't going to be happy until you've convinced yourself the painting you're looking for isn't here, so do it. Why don't you start with the bathroom? Then I'd like to bathe and change into some other clothes."

"I don't see anything wrong with what you have on." His gaze swept over her.

She looked down, not surprised to see that her nipples were hard in response to his look and now pressed against the thin material of her bra and shirt. She cursed her body for betraying her around him.

"I think I can dispense with searching the bathroom for a painting," he said, smiling smugly at her. He probably thought she enjoyed the kiss. Well, he was wrong. She was just playing along, letting him think he had her under his spell. No matter what her body thought, she was too smart to fall for anything Landry Jones was offering. But it did still annoy her the way he'd reacted when he thought she was a virgin.

She took some clothing from the chest of drawers—a pair of cropped pants, a shirt and some of the undergarments her mother had purchased for her back in South Dakota. She didn't feel safe in the skimpy underthings she'd bought since being in Florida.

As she shot a glance at Landry, she wasn't surprised to find he'd been watching her. He was looking smug, as if he knew why she'd chosen clothing that covered more of her body. What arrogance.

She groaned and stalked into the bathroom, closing the door and locking it. She could hear him searching the apartment and closed her eyes for a moment, imagining him going through the chest of drawers and her thong underwear.

Reminding herself that Landry in her underwear drawer was the least of her worries, she opened her eyes and reached in to turn on the shower—and screamed.

Chapter Ten

Landry practically flew into the bathroom, throwing open the door and almost knocking Willa down as he burst in, weapon drawn.

The bathroom was small and it only took him an instant to see that none of Freddy D.'s men were hiding in it. He heard a soft rustle and looked toward the bathtub.

The shower curtain was partially drawn back—just enough that he couldn't miss what was lying in the tub.

He flinched at the sight of the huge snake coiled in the bottom of the bathtub. He gently stepped back, putting Willa behind him as he did so. The snake was watching him through narrow slits, its tongue flicking from its wide flat head.

He'd seen his share of rattlesnakes, but this one had to be over six feet long—and appeared ready to strike.

In one quick movement, he was through the bathroom door and had the door between he and Willa and the snake. He breathed a sigh of relief and turned to look at her.

Her face was stark white, her eyes wide and scared, her hands trembling.

"What was *that?*" she whispered.

He grinned. "Don't they have rattlesnakes in South Dakota?"

"Not that big."

He chuckled and looked around for something to get the snake out of her tub.

"How did it get in there?"

"It came up through the pipes." He turned to look at her. She didn't really believe that, did she?

She'd sat down on the end of the bed but instead of looking scared, she looked angry. "It's whoever shot at me in the trees."

He didn't correct her as he opened the broom closet in the kitchen and pulled out a mop with a strip of sponge held in by eight inches of metal.

"What are you going to do?" she asked, sounding scared again as he passed her.

"I'm going to get the snake out of the tub, unless you want to shower with it." He opened the bathroom door quietly and slipped into the bathroom, moving behind the shower curtain. He could hear the snake trying to get out of the high old-fashioned tub. He took a breath and drew back the shower curtain with one hand, the mop handle in the other.

The snake turned at the sound, but Landry was faster. He slammed down the base of the mop, pinning the snake's head to the bottom of the tub, then gingerly he reached in and grabbed the snake behind the head and picked it up.

It twisted in his grasp. It was one heavy snake. As he stepped out of the bathroom, Willa let out a startled cry.

"Is it dead?"

"Not hardly." He moved to the back window near the couch, opened the window and pushed out the screen. Standing on the couch, he raised the snake and slid it through the open window, grabbing its tail to slow its fall as the snake disappeared.

"You let it go?" She sounded horrified.

"It was just a snake," he said, stepping down off the couch. "No reason to kill it."

Willa stared at him as if she'd never seen Landry Jones before. What kind of man couldn't kill a rattlesnake?

"You can take your bath now," he said.

She stared at him a moment longer then turned toward the bathroom, a little leery of what else she might find in there. "Are you sure—"

"Would kind of be overkill to have anything else in there, don't you think?"

Still she looked around before she turned on the faucet. It was probably one of the faster showers she'd ever taken, quickly washing off the sand and salt, shampooing her short hair and rinsing off.

She dried herself and dressed, feeling better as if wearing armor in the old-lady bra and panties that came up to her waist could protect her from her emotions. She couldn't help but think about Landry Jones. Just about the time she thought she had him figured out, he surprised her.

She gazed at her image in the mirror, dressed in the capris and tea-length sleeved blouse. She looked like the virgin she was, she thought with a self-deprecating smile.

As she stepped out of the bathroom, she found Landry standing by her bed holding a framed photograph. "These your parents?"

It was all she could do not to stomp over to him and snatch it from him. He already knew too much about her. "Yes."

"You grew up on a farm?" He seemed interested. Then she remembered that he was probably just wondering if she'd shipped some of her paintings home.

She walked over and took the photograph from him, unable to resist tracing her fingers over her father's face before setting it back down, then changing her mind and sticking it faceup in the top drawer.

"The paintings aren't in South Dakota," she snapped, angry with him for even pretending to care about her or her family.

"I wasn't—" He shook his head. "Never mind." He glanced around the apartment. "The painting isn't here."

She gave him a duh look. "I believe I already told you that."

He nodded. "Missouri, remember?"

She remembered.

"I grew up on a farm, too. Dirt-poor."

She felt her expression soften. “Me, too.”

He nodded and chewed at his cheek. “It was tough. I never wanted to be rich but I knew I had to do better than that.”

“I know what you mean.”

“You’re making it as an artist. That’s really something,” he said with what almost sounded like admiration in his voice.

“Well, I was *starting* to.”

He winced. “Sorry, but once this is over, you can get another studio, have a bunch more shows. It will be great.” He actually sounded like he believed that.

“Thanks. What about you?”

Landry sighed. “I really don’t know. I can’t see myself going back to it. Undercover work. I guess I didn’t realize how much I was starting to really fit into the role of bad guy. Maybe that’s what happened to Zeke. He got so used to playing the part, it became who he was.” Landry shrugged. “What happened with him changed things for me.”

She could see that. She just wasn’t sure in what way. They both started at the knock on the apartment door, then Odell’s voice. “Willie?”

“Willie?” Landry whispered.

“Willie?” Odell called again.

“Go ahead, answer him,” Landry whispered.

“Just a minute,” she called.

Landry smiled. “He’s going to think we’re in bed.”

She felt her face heat as she pushed past him and

went to the door. She'd rather take her chances with Odell than Landry anyday, she told herself.

"Hey," she said, smiling as she opened the door.

Odell seemed surprised by the greeting. True, she hadn't been even a little friendly before this. His gaze took her in. "You look...great."

Did she? She glanced toward the large stained mirror on the wall, surprised to see that her cheeks were flushed, her eyes bright. Past her reflection, she saw Landry's. He was watching her closely, grinning as if he knew exactly what had put the color in her cheeks, the gleam in her eyes.

She turned back to Odell and waited for him to remember what he was doing here.

"You're still up for a barbecue, right?" Odell hesitated and Willa felt Landry come up behind her. "I was about to put the steaks on."

"Steaks." Landry sounded so hopeful.

"I have them marinating."

"He's marinating the steaks," Landry said to her. Odell didn't notice but Willa could hear the sarcasm in Landry's voice.

"We'd love to join you," she said, knowing there was no graceful way out of this. Her other option was to spend the rest of the evening in this tiny apartment with Landry. Just the two of them.

"Great." Odell seemed surprised but happy they would be joining him.

"What can I bring?" Willa asked, then remembered how little food she had in the fridge. It had been just a reflex from South Dakota. "I have the makings for s'mores."

"Oh, girl, you'll kill me," Henri called up. "S'mores? I'm going to think I died and went to heaven. Can you believe I forgot chocolate? One of the basic food groups right up there with wine."

It sounded as if Henri had already been hitting the wine pretty hard.

"See you soon then," Odell said, glancing into the apartment. Actually glancing toward the bedroom.

Past Landry she saw that the covers were on the floor, the sheets rumpled. She stared back at the bed in shock.

Landry stepped in front of both hers and Odell's views, blocking the bed.

"Great," Odell repeated, sounding less enthusiastic as he turned to walk away. He spun back around almost at once though. "I'm sorry. I never caught your name," he said to Landry.

"Tim. Tim Patterson," Landry said without even blinking at the lie, and she was reminded that lying was second nature for him as an undercover cop. He held out his hand to Odell.

"Tim." Odell shook his hand then nodded to Willa. He looked suspicious. But then she thought everyone did.

She closed the door and leaned against it as she looked at Landry. "You did that to my bed?"

He grinned. "People believe what they see. You're safer if they think I'm your lover and I'm only interested in ravishing your body."

She hoped he didn't see her shiver at the thought.

"At least he has steak," Landry said. "So where is your other island mate? Blossom?"

"She's a teenage film and TV star," Willa said.

"Really?" He sounded interested. "I hope she's coming to the barbecue."

"I'm sure you do."

He shook his head. "I only have eyes for you, darlin'. Anyway, I'm more interested in who was shooting at you earlier than I am in a movie star."

Right.

SHE WENT into the tiny kitchen and got everything she needed for the s'mores. She could hear Landry in the tub. She tried not to imagine him naked.

When she had everything together, she heard the water shut off. A few moments later he came out wearing nothing but a towel wrapped around his waist. She looked away. Just not quick enough. Something burned in his gaze. Desire?

She felt her cheeks flush at the heat of his gaze and turned away for fear he might see the same in her eyes. She caught her reflection again in the antique mirror hanging on the living room wall and saw that she looked...happy. Or at least excited. Both were dangerous.

Suddenly Landry appeared in the mirror as he stepped up behind her. He slipped his arm around her neck from behind. She froze. His hand hovered for a moment then touched the collar of her shirt as he moved closer until his body was warm against hers. She felt his breath on her neck, the soft touch of his lips making the tiny hairs lift and her skin ripple with gooseflesh.

She held her breath as he straightened her collar, his fingers brushing over the skin below her collarbone.

"There," he said meeting her gaze in the mirror. "That looks better."

He held her gaze for a moment longer then returned to the bedroom and without closing the door, dressed in shorts and a T-shirt and his deck shoes. "Ready?"

She felt bereft at the loss of his touch. She dropped her gaze, not wanting him to see what he was doing to her but afraid he knew only too well. Why hadn't she fessed up to her lack of sexual experience? It was certainly nothing to be ashamed of. Was she afraid he would take advantage of it? Or because from the way he'd acted she feared he wouldn't?

"SO YOU'RE BLOSSOM," Landry said a few minutes later when they joined the other residents down by the pool where Odell had pulled up several tables and some chairs and had a grill going. Loud obnoxious music blared from Blossom's room across the pool.

Blossom gave Landry a bored look from eyes rimmed in charcoal. She appeared drugged as she slouched in one of the lawn chairs and pouted behind a wall of kinky dyed-black hair. She wore the same black outfit she had on earlier. Willa wondered if everything the girl owned was black.

"Her agent forced her to come here for some downtime," Henri said, and chuckled as she lifted her glass of wine in a toast. "There are worse places to be. I've just never found them." She laughed and downed her wine.

Odell reached for the wine bottle and quickly refilled her glass, then turned to offer some to Willa and Landry.

"You wouldn't have a beer, would you?" Landry asked.

"In the cooler," Henri said. "I always like to be prepared. Bloody Marys in the morning."

Landry popped the top on a beer and offered it to Willa. She shook her head and held up her drink of preference. "I brought bottled water, thanks."

"Bottled water," Landry said. "That's my girl."

She ignored him and took a sip of her water to cool herself down. What was Landry up to? She was having trouble believing this was about finding whoever had shot at her earlier today. She suspected there was a whole lot more to it.

"This is really nice of you," Landry said as Odell cooked the steaks. "We hate to eat all your food."

"I have the supply boat coming back tomorrow. This island might be isolated, but there isn't any reason not to be civilized," he said, and looked over at Willa.

Henri finished off the wine and went to get another bottle, weaving as she walked back to her apartment. Blossom continued to sulk in her lawn chair.

Willa tried to imagine which of the three could shoot at her, let alone put a huge rattlesnake in her bathtub.

"She's getting over a broken heart," Odell said, watching Henri stumble into her apartment.

"Willie tells me you're writing a book," Landry said, sipping at his beer and watching Odell cook the steaks.

"Did she?" Odell looked over at her. "I'm still at that stage where I'm not completely sure what I want to write about."

"I thought you were doing it on this place," Landry said. "Cape Diablo and the Villa Santiago. It's definitely creepy enough. So what is your theory?"

"My theory?" Odell asked.

"On what happened to Andres and..." Landry looked to Willa.

"Medina," she provided.

"Medina and the other two kids?"

Odell looked uncomfortable as he glanced at Willa. "I think they were murdered here, their bodies disposed of on the property."

Willa shivered, remembering the night before when Odell had buried something on the property.

"Could this place be any creepier?" Henri asked, returning with another bottle of wine. She handed it to Landry, smiling suggestively as she said, "Be a love and open that for me, will ya?"

Landry returned Henri's smile and took the corkscrew from her and slowly opened the bottle while Henri watched, as if in fascination. Willa found herself watching, as well. His movements were skilled, his hands large and nicely shaped, the backs tanned from the sun, his fingers working the cork slowly, gently, patiently from the bottle.

He would be that kind of lover, Willa thought, then looked away, shocked by the very idea.

"Odell tells us you're here because of a broken heart?" Landry said to the redhead.

Henri nodded. "He turned out to be a real bastard."

"All men are bastards," Landry said. "It's only the degree of bastard that separates us." He shot a look at Willa. "Isn't that right, darlin'?"

"Absolutely," she said. "And if anyone knows, it's you, *sweetheart.*"

He grinned meeting her gaze. "You can see why I love her."

Henri laughed and took the glass of wine Landry gave her before stumbling into her lawn chair again. Blossom hadn't moved but she did seem to be watching everything. Just as Willa had seen her apparently listening to everything the evening before.

The steaks ready, Odell handed everyone a plate. "It's not fancy," he said when he gave Willa hers. "Steak and salad. That's as fancy as we get out here in the middle of nowhere. Kind of like out West. Montana, Wyoming, the Dakotas. Not that I've ever been there." He smiled at her.

She took the plate, her fingers trembling. She hadn't told him she was from South Dakota, had she? Or was he just making small talk?

She glanced at Landry.

If he'd heard, he gave no indication. He was busy

cutting his steak. He took a bite. "Great steaks, Odell. You'll have to give me your marinade recipe."

Odell smiled and said, "Thanks," but Willa could see that he didn't like Landry. Not that she could blame him.

Henri didn't eat much of her dinner but was all over the s'mores. She was letting Landry make her another one when Odell touched Willa's shoulder and motioned her toward the open door of his apartment.

"Would you mind helping me a minute?" he asked quietly.

Landry and Henri didn't seem to notice. Blossom was watching them with apparent disinterest.

"Sure," Willa said, and stepped into his apartment.

He moved to the back where there was a small kitchenette. The moment she joined him, he turned to face her. "How long have you known him?"

Willa blinked, not sure at first who he was talking about.

"Tim," Odell said. "How long have you known him?"

"Not that long," she admitted. "Why?"

"I just have a bad feeling about him," Odell said. "I know it sounds silly. But he feels…dangerous."

She couldn't have agreed more. "Dangerous?" she repeated, just for something to say.

Odell grasped her forearm. "Don't trust him. I'm serious. I don't think he's right for you." He took his hand back quickly as if he realized he was overstepping his bounds. "I'm sorry. It isn't any of my business. You're obviously attracted to him. Maybe I'm all wrong about him."

"No," she said, and quickly added, "I appreciate your concern. I'll be careful."

"You just don't seem like the type of woman who would go for that kind of man. You know, the crude, aggressive type." Was that how Odell saw Landry? "He isn't the one who hurt you, is he?"

Had she told Odell the same story she'd told Gator? Or had Odell gotten his information from Gator? She really had to try to remember who she was telling what to. Keeping track of her lies was exhausting.

"No, Tim's not the one who was abusive to me," she said.

Odell nodded, but he didn't look like he believed it.

Henri called that they'd better get back out to the fire or all of the s'mores would be gone. She sounded drunk.

Without another word Odell returned to poolside. Willa glanced around his kitchen, peeked into the bedroom, then wandered back out. Was Odell really who he said he was and was his concern real? Or was there a gun with a silencer hidden somewhere in his apartment, a gunny sack that once held a poisonous snake? She couldn't help but wonder if what Odell really wanted was Landry out of her life. But why?

Back outside, Willa found herself watching Landry. It wasn't until she saw him talking to Blossom that she realized what he was up to.

He'd said they had to find out who was trying to kill her. She just assumed he meant to stop them. But now she realized that if one of these people was willing to kill her before they got the disk then Landry was thinking they already had the painting and the disk and they were just tying up loose ends.

"You all right, darlin'?" Landry asked.

She swore some times it felt as if he could read her mind. He kissed her neck and whispered, "You aren't jealous, are you? I saw the way you were looking at me. If looks could kill."

She groaned. She hated being so transparent.

He chuckled. "Let's go somewhere private," he said just loud enough for everyone to hear.

Willa felt her face flame as he pulled her to her feet.

"Thanks for dinner," Landry said with a grin. "I know you'll understand if Willie and I call it a night."

Henri raised her wineglass in a silent salute.

Odell said nothing, his gaze on Willa. He'd been watching her all evening. And she would wager he knew she was from South Dakota. She shivered as she climbed the stairs ahead of Landry and wasn't even surprised when he cupped her buttock on the way up and swept her into his arms as they both stumbled into her apartment.

It was what he said once they were inside that surprised her.

Chapter Eleven

"Henri is as sober as I am," Landry said as he locked the door behind them. "And if she's getting over a heartbreak I'll eat your underwear."

Willa ignored that. "You think Henri is the one who shot at me, the one who put the snake in my bathtub?" she asked incredulously.

Landry was checking the apartment. For killers? Or snakes? "She could be just setting up Odell," he said as he checked the bathroom. "You know, pretending she's really drunk so he'll make his move." Landry shrugged. "She's wasting her time, though. Odell's not interested in her." His gaze settled on Willa's face. "He wants you."

"Not in the way you think," she said. "He let it slip tonight that he knows I'm from South Dakota. I never told him that. He must have gotten it from the newspaper articles, which means he knows who I am."

"That doesn't make him the shooter," Landry said. "Come on. You saw what he buried behind the villa. The guy's afraid of his shadow. He is no snake handler. No, trust me, the guy's got the hots for you."

"Do you always have to be so crude?"

He smiled as if he thought it was part of his charm. "Now, Blossom is something else. She looks like she could wrestle a snake. You ever see her in anything on TV or the big screen?"

Willa shook her head. "She acts like she's bored but I saw her watching everyone."

Landry nodded, eyeing her with what could have been respect. "So you *were* paying attention." He glanced at his watch. "We should try to get some sleep."

She glanced toward the bed.

"I'll take the couch," he said, as if reading her mind again.

"Fine," she said, heading for the bedroom.

"Leave the door open," he ordered.

She turned to look at him.

"In case someone tries to get you in the middle of the night," he said, and grinned. "I'll wake you when it's time to go."

Like she could sleep knowing he was in the next room, she thought after brushing her teeth, washing her face and applying a light night cream—her usual routine which she was determined to keep no matter how many killers were after her.

She had thought about changing into her longest nightshirt in the bathroom but since she and Landry would be leaving sometime in the middle of the night, she dressed in her darkest-colored jeans and shirt to be ready. Safer that way for everyone.

The living room light was out when she came from the bathroom. She couldn't see Landry on the couch but she knew he was there. Just as she knew his eyes were on her.

She slipped between the covers and turned out the light, pitching the apartment into darkness. He'd indicated that he didn't make love to virgins, and he was convinced she was one. She should have felt safe. But she feared it wasn't Landry Jones's willpower she had to worry about.

When she closed her eyes, she saw him grinning down at her as his lips moved closer and closer until he was kissing her again.

LANDRY HEARD her moan in her sleep and tiptoed to the bedroom door. A shaft of moonlight cut through a crack in the curtains and fell over the rounded curves beneath the thin sheet.

Watching her sleep, he had a hard time getting enough breath. The woman had no idea just how irresistible she was. Or how much danger she was in. She was determined that she could take care of herself. He shook his head at that foolish notion.

So far he hadn't seen T or Worm. He figured they could be underground until all this blew over since both had been made when they'd killed the two police officers at the safe house and let Willa St. Clair get away.

Suddenly he felt as if someone had knocked the air

out of him. He stumbled from her bedroom doorway, the words echoing in his head.

Let her get away.

He swore. Of course that's what Freddy D. had ordered T and Worm to do. Let her get away so she could lead them to the disk. Freddy D. was too smart to use muscle like T and Worm to go after Willa St. Clair. He'd put someone with more finesse on her if he really wanted to catch her.

Someone like Landry himself.

He stepped to the window. Odell's light was on in his apartment. The poolside area where they'd had the barbecue was empty, bottles and glasses still on the tables, but no sign of Henri. Or Blossom.

Was it possible he was being played? His heart beat a little faster. Was it the only reason he was still alive? Still free?

He felt like a puppet. Someone was pulling his strings. He thought about Zeke trying to kill him at the gallery. It hadn't made any sense. It still didn't. Unless he and Zeke had both been set up that night. If Zeke thought Landry was the dirty cop, thought he was lying about having the painting and the disk, thought maybe he'd turned and was either taking the disk to Freddy D. or selling it to Freddy D.'s enemies.

Closing the blind, Landry went back to the couch, his mind whirling. The disk would be worth a small fortune if sold to the right people. If Zeke thought that Landry really had turned….

Landry knew he'd rather believe that than believe his friend had been the dirty cop.

The front door and the windows were all locked. He was a light sleeper. He'd hear anyone who tried to enter the apartment. He told himself that Willa was safe.

Lying down on the couch, he closed his eyes, trying to slow down his thoughts. Simon had gotten the disk from a reliable source. It would have valuable information about Freddy D.'s organization. But it would also have a list of who worked for him—including any cops.

Landry had to find that disk. Not just to prove his own innocence but to prove Zeke's. Zeke and Simon couldn't have died for nothing. If there was a dirty cop in Freddy's D.'s organization, it couldn't have been Zeke.

Music started to play overhead. He could hear the soft scuff of feet. Someone was dancing. The old woman. Alma Garcia. She'd said something else that Landry hadn't told Willa, something that had shaken him.

She'd asked him if he'd come back to kill her.

He must have slept some. The music was no longer playing. Nor could he hear anyone dancing. Getting up, he checked outside. It was still dark, the moon high.

No lights shone in Odell's apartment. Opening the door, Landry glanced below the balcony. Nor were any lights burning in Henri's or Blossom's apartments.

Not that one or all them might not be wide-awake. Would Freddy D. trust just one person with going after Willa and the disk? Even if that one person was Landry

Jones? Landry didn't think so. If he were Freddy D., he would have sent a backup.

He stepped back into the apartment, quietly closing the door, and tiptoed into Willa's room, aware that Henri's and Blossom's smaller apartments were just below and the floor creaked.

"Ready?" he whispered next to Willa's ear. She smelled heavenly. His lips brushed her skin. Soft.

She came awake in an instant, looked scared, then annoyed to see him. Nothing new there.

She nodded, threw back the sheet and swung her legs over the side. It took a few moments to put on her tennis shoes. He was glad to see that she'd chosen dark jeans and a long-sleeved dark-colored shirt. She snugged a navy baseball cap down over her head and stood.

"The keys to the storage unit?" he whispered.

She held them up, along with a small penlight. She had to be kidding.

He handed her a real flashlight from his backpack and took the extra one for himself.

She pocketed her penlight and gave him a look that said she didn't like him much.

Better that way, he thought as he motioned for her to be as quiet as possible. She followed behind him, barely making a sound. At the door, he opened it and peered out again.

No sign of anyone. He led the way down the stairs and through the archway. Once past the house and under the canopy of the trees there was no light from the moon. He stopped to listen to make sure they hadn't been followed. He could hear Willa's soft breaths. He reached for her hand; it felt cool to his touch.

Willa felt his fingers search out her hand. She tried not to flinch at his unexpected touch. Or shiver at the tingle of that same touch as his fingers tightened around hers.

She could feel the dampness, hear the breeze moving through the trees high above them, and smell the Gulf.

Landry stopped, pulled her close and for one crazy moment, she thought he was going to kiss her. Instead, he appeared to be listening, as if he feared they'd been followed. All she could hear was the sound of her own pulse pounding in her ears.

After a moment, he drew her deeper into the trees. She could hear the surf ahead. The trees opened. Moonlight spilled over the water. Waves curled white and broke on the beach. The tide was out again.

Landry moved quickly to the brush. She heard the scrape of metal over the sound of the surf breaking on the rocks behind her farther up the beach.

He pulled a small boat from the bushes and motioned for her to get in.

She hesitated but only for a moment, then stepped into the boat. Landry pushed it out and hopped in. A wave crashed over the front of the bow sending up cold spray.

She shivered as Landry paddled away from the island before starting the motor. The boat purred through the moonlight. She watched Landry as he worked his way past mangrove island after mangrove island, surprised how at home he looked on the water. She wouldn't have been surprised if Landry was at home in almost any situation.

When she glanced back toward the island, she saw a figure at the edge of the trees.

"Landry," she said over the putt of the outboard. She motioned back toward the shore.

He turned, eyes narrowing as the figure melted back into the vegetation. "Did you see who it was?" he asked after they'd rounded one of the other islands.

She shook her head, hugging herself. Someone had followed them. Someone knew they'd left the island.

For a long while, she watched behind them, expecting to see another boat on the moon-slick surface or hear another motor. But there was nothing but islands and the gentle rock of the boat to the steady throb of the motor to lull her.

She must have closed her eyes, lying back in the boat, looking up at the moon riding high in the sky. As she drifted off, she tried not to think about what would happen once Landry had the painting and the disk.

Her eyes opened as she became aware that the boat had slowed. Landry brought the bow up to the dock. She grabbed hold of the ladder and held on as Landry hopped out and tied up the boat before reaching for her hand.

They walked through Everglades City, the town deserted at this hour of the night. Willa felt as if they might be the only two people still alive anywhere. It was a strange feeling, this closeness to Landry, this feeling that they were in this together.

She knew it wouldn't last but for tonight she breathed in the exotic scents, Landry Jones's among them, and didn't think about tomorrow. Or even the rest of tonight.

As they walked, she noticed Landry turning to look over his shoulder just as she had been doing for days. But she saw no one. She heard no other boat or even a car. It was off-season and most of the houses along the water were boarded-up and empty.

When they reached the storage facility, she took the keys from her pocket. The units were one long row of metal compartments behind a chain-link fence. She went to the gate and used a key to get them inside, locking it behind them.

Several large outdoor lights shone at each end of the property. Only moonlight lit the middle section and only on the east side. It was pitch-black on the west side where her unit was located. They stayed to the shadows, Landry watching behind them as she moved along the shell lane. She started at the sound of a dog barking in the distance.

She used another key to open the padlock on the door to her storage unit. It made a soft click. She froze, listened, then stepped aside as Landry rolled the door upward, the sound loud as a gunshot.

They quickly stepped in, closed the door and turned on the flashlights Landry had supplied.

The storage unit was nearly empty. Only a half-dozen boxes sat in one corner. Willa quickly moved to them not sure what they would find since all of the boxes had been packed by the police.

Landry pulled a knife and cut the tape on each box. She stared at the knife, remembering her cut art supply box, then shaking off her suspicion, began to go through the contents quickly, hoping she would find the painting or a disk—and yet afraid what would happen once she did.

It didn't take long to go through the six boxes that she'd left here only days before. The painting wasn't there.

She closed the last box and turned to look at Landry. He'd been going through the boxes after her. He swore as he looked through the last one, then he glanced up at her, a look of both disappointment and fear on his face.

"It's not here," she said because someone needed to say it.

He nodded. "You packed it for the show. The gallery owner must still have it."

From his tone she knew going anywhere near St. Pete Beach would be dangerous. And not just for her. Landry was more well-known there than she was. He would be at an even greater risk.

"I can go try to find it," she said, realizing that on some level she believed his story about Zeke's death. Otherwise why risk her life to save his?

He smiled and turned off his flashlight. Hers was pointed at the concrete floor, leaving his handsome face in shadow, his eyes looking even darker than usual.

"There is no way I'd let you go alone," he said.

"If you're worried about me not coming back with the painting—"

"It's not that. It's too dangerous for you to go at all, let alone by yourself."

She felt a prickling of suspicion. "You want to go alone?"

"You can call Evan, tell him to cooperate with me," Landry said.

She stared at him, hating that he could so quickly make her feel uncertain of him.

"Isn't it possible that I want to protect you?" He was staring at her as if it made a difference what she thought.

Don't do this, Willa. Don't trust him. You know he'll only end up hurting you.

She couldn't look into his face. She turned off her flashlight, pitching the inside of the storage unit into blackness. She could hear him breathing, knew he was close, closer than he'd been just moments before. She swallowed, her nerves raw with just the thought of him, her body alive with the thought of his touch.

"We should get back to the island," she said, her voice barely a whisper.

"Not yet." His voice was rough with emotion and so close, she felt his breath warm her cheek.

She jumped at the brush of fingertips along her arm, then his arm was around her waist, dragging her to him as his mouth dropped unerringly to hers.

He groaned as if kissing her had been the least of his plans. She could barely breathe, the way he held her so tightly against him, her breasts crushed to his chest. He parted her lips with his tongue, and she opened to him.

Her heart was pounding so hard, she knew he had to feel it in his chest. Her body melted against his, her arms going around his neck as the kiss deepened and her pulse made a buzzing sound in her ears.

He shifted his body, his hand slipping between them to cup her breast. Heat shot through her, her breast aching, her nipples hard as pebbles, sending a fire shooting through her veins straight to her center.

She moaned against his mouth as he thumbed the hard peak of her nipple, the pleasure almost unbearable. "Landry," she breathed against the hot pressure of his mouth.

Lifting her, he pressed her against the Sheetrock wall and shoved her shirt up to get to the old-lady bra she'd put on earlier. He jerked it up and freed her breasts in one shift motion. She leaned her head back, arching her body against him as the night air blew across her bare breasts, dimpling her flesh an instant before she felt the hot wet suction of his mouth on her nipple.

She gasped, the intensity of the sensation making her dizzy. She could feel his fingers working at the zipper on her black jeans, feel his hardness through his own jeans against her bare belly.

Without warning, he stopped, cursed and drew back, his hands on her hips the only thing holding her up since her legs had gone to rubber.

She let out a small cry of frustration and fear that he wouldn't continue. She couldn't see his face—just hear him breathing hard. She wanted him like she'd never wanted anything in her life.

"Tell me about all the men you've had," he whispered.

She began to cry, great big tears silently rolling down her cheeks.

He leaned into her again, his lips brushing across hers, but she knew whatever had possessed him moments ago had passed. He'd changed his mind. She wanted to beat his chest with her fists. She wanted to beg him to take her.

He gently kissed her lips, then her tears. "Not here. Not like this. Not your first time."

She started to protest but he covered her lips with his in a silencing kiss, then pulled back as if he heard something. He turned on the flashlight, pointing it at their feet, but his gaze was on her face.

"Someday you'll thank me," he said as he laid down the flashlight, the beam shooting across the floor to the back of the shedlike room.

He reached to button her jeans but she pushed his hand away as she pulled her bra down over her breasts, covering herself, fingers trembling as she fought to get her balance and jeans buttoned. She'd never slept with a man because she'd never wanted one badly enough. Until now.

The faint clink of metal on metal made them both freeze. Landry quickly motioned to her to be quiet as he reached down and shut off his flashlight. A clank of metal on metal. Someone had just come in through the gate to the storage units.

Landry moved quickly to the large door and lifted it a few feet off the ground. Moonlight bled into the opening. He checked outside, then motioned for her to slip through and followed her. She heard him quietly close and snap the padlock into place, then move along the shadowed side toward the front of the property, motioning for her to wait.

He returned a few moments later. "It's an armed security guard," he whispered, and motioned for her to follow him toward the back of the property.

Her heart lodged in her throat. If they were caught, Landry would go to jail. She would go to another safe house. Neither of them would be safe. In fact, she suspected they wouldn't last long, given the powerful people after them.

A breeze stirred the palms that lined the back of the chain-link fence. She could hear mosquitoes buzzing next to her ear and smell the swampy stew that bordered the property. In the moonlight, she caught a glimpse of one alligator, then another. The tourist wild-animal park she'd seen was right next door.

Back here the fence surrounding the storage units was ten feet high but there was no razor wire along the top. There were just alligators lounging in the swamp on the other side of the fence.

Willa saw at once what Landry had planned and balked at even the idea. "Alligators," she whispered, just in case he hadn't noticed.

He knelt down, his fingers weaved together as he motioned for her to put her foot in for a boost up the fence. "Trust me," he whispered.

Right. She heard the sound of footfalls coming along the edge of the storage units and quickly weighed her options before putting her foot into his hands. He boosted her up. She grabbed hold of the fence and climbed to the top, swung a leg over and teetered there for a moment before gingerly working her way down the other side, all the while keeping an eye on the alligators.

Landry bounded up the fence, over the top and down the other side. He caught her as she dropped to the ground. She heard the scurry of the alligators nearest the fence and for a moment she thought they were scurrying after her instead of away.

"Come on." Landry took her hand, dragging her through the swamp toward the small shack that acted as a ticket booth for the wildlife exhibit. At one point, he stopped and pulled her down next to a large fake rock. She held her breath, listening not just for the security guard but for any alligators sneaking up on them. Off to her left, she saw a huge gator yawn, his massive jaws opening and finally closing again.

They slipped under the gate by the ticket booth and ran across the street, losing themselves in the shadows of the buildings as they wove through the small residential area.

"Neither of us can go to St. Pete Beach," he said when they finally quit running. He'd stopped by a fishing shack near the canal. The area was a web of canals. The night was deathly quiet. No lights or vehicles anywhere. "They'll be waiting for us." His gaze met hers in the darkness, his dark eyes shining. "We have to try to get the paintings sent to us."

She hated the thought of involving Evan Charles in all this. Keeping her voice down, she asked, "Are you sure the police or Freddy D. don't already have the disk?"

"If the police did, then Freddy and his crew would be behind bars. No one would want us dead. Just the opposite."

"And if Freddy has it?"

He shook his head. "If he did then he wouldn't have any reason to want you dead. If anything, he'd want to keep you alive so you could testify against me."

He touched her cheek, his hand cool, his touch making her shiver but not from the cold. "Trust me. The disk hasn't been found. That's why you and I are still alive. That's why we have to contact the gallery owner—and not go there. Come on." He took her hand. "I saw a pay phone back by that closed motel."

Pop. Wood splintered on the shack wall beside her. Landry knocked her to the ground, landing hard on top of her and rolled them both down the slope toward the water. *Pop. Pop.*

The last thing she heard was Landry whisper next to her ear, "Hold your breath."

Chapter Twelve

They hit the water.

Landry pulled her under, dragging her deeper and deeper, forcing her to swim after him, the water growing colder and colder as they dove down toward the bottom.

Her head buzzed. She needed desperately to take a breath but he had a death grip on her wrist. Even if she thought about going to the surface and taking her chances against the would-be killer with the gun, Landry wasn't letting her go.

Suddenly he stopped swimming and pulled her upward. Her eyes were open but all she could see was blackness as her head broke the surface. She gasped for breath, her lungs burning. Her free hand struck something hard.

"Quiet," Landry whispered and she realized they'd come up under one of the docks along the canal.

She sucked in air, her body trembling from fear and lack of oxygen, as she treaded water, unable to touch bottom. The water was cold and she kept going under.

Landry pulled her to him, holding her up so her head was above water. His body felt warm and strong. She let him take her weight and fought the need to cry. She'd gone twenty-five years without anyone trying to kill her and now every time she turned around someone was shooting at her or putting snakes in her bathtub. She wasn't sure how much more of this she could take.

As if Landry sensed her despair, he pulled her closer, pressing his cheek to hers, holding her gently. She wrapped her arms around him and closed her eyes.

Overhead someone stepped onto the dock. It rocked, making the water under the dock splash. Landry pulled her out deeper into the water until they were almost to the end of the dock, never letting go of her.

The footsteps were slow, purposeful. Did the killer know they were under the dock? Had he seen them? The dock pushed down as the would-be killer walked to the end, leaving little space above their heads for air. But in Landry's arms, Willa felt safe. The irony of it wasn't lost on her.

She leaned back, trying not to panic. Landry was still holding her, his touch calming. She thanked God she wasn't alone or she knew she would have been dead. He'd saved her again. Her heart swelled, tears burning her eyes.

The dock buoyed upward as the footsteps retreated back down the dock.

They waited, listening. Water lapped softly at the sides of the dock. A dog barked in the distance. Finally there was the sound of a car engine, the crunch of gravel beneath the tires and then the growl of the car's motor dying away in the distance.

"Wait here for just a second," Landry whispered and disappeared below the water.

He was gone for more than a second. She was getting ready to panic when he reappeared.

"Looks clear. Take my hand."

She did as he told her, swimming down before heading again to the surface. They came up on the lee side of the dock out of the moonlight. Quietly they swam to shore.

She was shaking hard now, the cold, the fear, all her adrenaline long gone. He helped her up onto the shore. Her legs trembled. She stumbled and would have gladly sat down for a while but he dragged her up along the side of the fish shack, then across the street, moving fast.

It would be light soon, surprising her how much time had gone by since they'd left the island.

The phone booth was an old-fashioned one, the kind that were hard to find, thanks to cell phones and vandalism. Landry dug out a handful of coins and dropped them on the metal tray.

Keeping the door open so the overhead light didn't come on, she dialed Information, waited and then asked for Evan Charles's number. She repeated it out loud to Landry, then still shaking, dialed Evan's number, using the coins Landry supplied as he stood guard. The answering machine picked up after the fifth ring.

"Evan. It's Willa St. Clair. I need to talk to you. If you're there, could you—"

"Willa?" Evan sounded groggy.

"I'm sorry to call you at this hour but I need your help."

"Oh girl, I heard what happened. It's in the all papers. You must be scared to death, sweetie. Was it just awful?"

She had to smile, imagining him sitting up in bed now, eating up the drama. "Evan, what did you do with my paintings that didn't sell?"

"You need money. Of course you do. I told you I could sell them if you let me keep them in the shop."

Her heart fell. "Is that what you did?"

"Of course not. You told me you wanted to wait until you could have another show and we agreed that would give you the most play."

She breathed a sigh of relief. "How many are left?"

"Not even half a dozen."

Landry was motioning to her. "Evan, was there one painting that didn't get hung at the show?"

"Oh, sweetie, I just feel awful about that. I found it later when I went to pack up the others. Do you hate me?"

"Of course not." She nodded to Landry. Relief washed over him, softening the hard lines of his face. He couldn't have been more handsome.

"Can you just describe the painting for me?" she asked, and listened while he confirmed that it was the one they had all been looking for.

"It had a tear in the backing, I guess that's why my assistant didn't put it up," Evan said. "I am just sick about it. I'm positive it would have sold, sweetie."

"It's not a problem, really. I have a terribly big favor

to ask of you. Would it be possible for you to send me the paintings without anyone knowing? I could give you an address."

"Not on his home line, in case it's tapped," Landry whispered.

"Could I call you back on your cell and tell you where to send them?" she asked.

"Oh, such intrigue. I'm just shivering all over," he cried. He rattled off his cell number, Willa repeating it.

"I'll call you right back."

"I'll get a pen and paper. Don't worry, sweetie, I'll destroy the evidence. I'll shred it. Or burn it. If you want, I'll shred it and eat it with a nice marinara sauce."

She hung up, half shaking her head. Evan was such a trip. She adored him. She just prayed that she wasn't endangering him.

"Wait," Landry said as she started to dial Evan's cell. "The safest way to do this is have Evan send the box by special courier to the marina so Bull can bring it out tomorrow when he brings the rest of the supplies. If he does it tonight, it will get here in time."

She nodded and called Evan's cell, gave him the address for Bull. "Address the box to Cara Wilson. That's the name I'm using."

"I'll do it right now. Not to worry. You really must let me know how this all turns out. I'll just be on pins and needles until I hear."

She promised, hung up and looked at Landry. This was almost over but she knew her life would never be the same.

There was one regret she was determined she wouldn't have when it was all over, she told herself as she leaned into Landry and kissed him.

"You all right?" Landry asked, seeming surprised.

She just looked at him. Was she all right? He had to be kidding. She was soaked to the skin, half-drowned, some kind of seaweed stuff in her hair and at least one person was trying to kill her—more than likely more.

He smiled and picked something green from her hair. "Think you can make it back to the boat?"

Like she had a choice. She nodded. The sky behind them paled as they reached the boat. She'd half expected someone to be waiting for them in ambush but apparently no one knew what Landry's boat looked like, and there were dozens of boats tied up along the canal.

She climbed in, surprised that she was starting to get her sea legs. He untied the boat and stepped in after her, quickly starting the motor and turning the bow out toward the watery horizon.

He tossed her an old towel from the bottom of the boat. It smelled of gas and oil. She didn't even care. She wrapped it around her and slid down in the boat. Sleep took her at once, dragging her down into a dreamless cold darkness.

She woke with a start, blinded by the light and jarred awake as the boat hit the sand. Struggling to sit up, she looked around. They were back on the island. She was awed and surprised that Landry had managed to get them back here alive. Daylight broke over the tops of the mangrove islands to the east. She felt as if she'd been dragged through the mud, like an alley cat sneaking home after a rough night on the streets.

As she turned to look at Landry, she saw the blood. "My God, you're shot!"

Landry smiled at the concern in her voice. "It's all right," he said as he stepped out into the water and pulled the boat partway up on shore. "It's just a flesh wound."

She climbed out, looking unsteady and a little green around the gills. "Why didn't you tell me you were shot?" She sounded angry now.

"It's no big deal. Anyway, what would you have done? You aren't one of those women who faint at the sight of blood, are you?" He reached for her as she seemed to wobble. "Oh, hell," he said as she sank to the sand.

He dropped beside her and forced her head between her knees. "Take deep breaths."

She was crying softly, gasping for breath. "My mother wanted me to be a nurse."

He laughed, and rubbed the back of her neck with his palm. "Yeah, you would have made a great nurse." When she was breathing normally, he hid the boat in the bushes again and then helped her up. "Can you walk?"

She looked offended. "Of course I can walk." She glanced at his upper arm, the shirtsleeve soaked with blood, and started to go faint on him again.

"Come on," he said, leading her through the brush, using his uninjured arm to guide her. They had to bushwhack for a ways through the brush before they hit the trail, skirting around the swamp and unstable ground.

"Watch out. There are parts of this island that are like quicksand," he told her. "You wander in there and you're never coming out again."

He was glad to see that the tide was coming in, the waves washing away any sign of their footprints in the sand. Soon the small beach would be covered in water.

He'd had time to think about the attack at Everglades City. Whoever had seen them leave the island had to have contacted someone onshore. First the security guard at the storage facility. Then the shooter.

What bothered him was that the two incidents didn't seem connected. The guard hadn't seemed alarmed. He might have just been checking things after being called about a possible break-in.

The shooter was a whole other story. He'd tried to kill them both. One of Zeke's friends from the force? Definitely someone who didn't give a damn about the disk—and just wanted Landry dead.

Landry was sure he'd been the target. Willa's mistake was being with him. And here he'd thought he could protect her. The way things were going, he would get her killed.

But the painting was on its way. All they had to do was wait for Bull to bring it to them then get off this island. He thought about the person he and Willa had seen watching them leave the island. Was it possible they'd been followed?

He hadn't heard another boat but no reason to take a chance. On the way back to the villa, he took a detour. "Stay here," he whispered, and sneaked down to the old fisherman's dock and checked the boat motor. Ice-cold. The boat hadn't been out.

"What?" Willa said when he returned and they were headed for the villa again.

"Is there another boat on the island that you know of because that one hasn't been anywhere," he said.

She shook her head. "You think the person who saw us leave somehow contacted whoever was shooting at us? But there is no cell phone service out here."

He smiled. "Exactly. That's what makes me think there's a boat we don't know about."

The villa was silent as they slipped through the archway and made their way up to her apartment. Once inside, Landry locked the door.

Willa looked beat and worse there was something so endearing about her he just wanted to hold her and promise her that everything was going to be all right.

It was a promise he couldn't make though, and holding her right now when they were both feeling vulnerable was the last thing he should do.

He walked through the bedroom and turned on the water in the tub. She was still standing where he'd left her looking lost. He motioned her into the bathroom. "Strip down and get in there. You can get hypothermia even this far south, and right now you look like you might tip over at any moment." He stripped off his shirt.

Willa's eyes widened.

"Don't worry, I'm not getting in with you. I'm just going to clean up the wound and then go see if I can find another boat on the island. I'll lock the door as I leave. You get some rest. I'll be back before you know it."

She nodded and he turned his back to her. He cranked on some water in the sink and began to gingerly wash the flesh wound to his shoulder. This was the second bullet he'd taken in a matter of days. Not a good sign.

"There's a first-aid kit in the cabinet," she said behind him.

He opened the medicine cabinet over the sink and took out the box, amused to see what all was in it—including a note that read "Be careful. Love, Mom xoxox."

He smiled to himself as he took out the gauze and replaced the box, note and all.

Just before the mirror steamed completely over, he saw Willa slip out of her shirt and bra. He looked away, but not before he'd seen the pale creamy flesh of her breasts and remembered the warm soft weight of her breast in his palm. Just the sight of her half-naked sent a stab of desire through him like a hot knife blade.

He ducked his head, waiting until he heard her step into the tub and close the curtain before he looked up again. Fighting the urge to join her in the tub no matter what he'd said, he quickly cleaned the wound. It hurt like hell but it was exactly what he needed to exorcise the memory of Willa half-naked and remind him what was at stake here. He had to keep his mind on finding the disk. The last thing he needed was to let Willa St. Clair, South Dakota virgin, distract him.

The thought made him laugh. She more than distracted him.

"What's so funny?" she asked from in the tub.

"You, darlin'," he said as he shut off the water in the sink and covered the wound to his arm with the bandage before pulling on a clean shirt.

"I was just thinking about you and all those men you've been with," he said, and stepped out of the bathroom as the shower curtain opened a crack and a bar of soap flew past his head. He closed the door just in time, smiling to himself as the soap smacked the bathroom door.

In his duffel bag he took out his second gun, the one *with* the silencer, feeling surprisingly guilty. He'd had to do what needed to be done and yet… He stuck the weapon in the waistband of his shorts, covering it with the tail of his shirt.

He heard Willa get out of the tub to retrieve the soap as he left, locking the door behind him. The villa was quiet, no one apparently up yet, as he left. The sun rose behind the palms to the east in a burst of hot orange.

As Landry walked, he mulled over the same thoughts that had been haunting him since they'd left Everglades City. What if he was wrong about being the target? But who would want Willa dead? It made no sense.

If his theory was right Freddy D. had made sure both he and Willa were free so they could find the disk for him. Even Zeke's buddies wouldn't kill Willa.

So who did that leave?

Someone who didn't want the disk to ever be found. Or for Landry or Willa to live long enough to talk.

Landry swore as he circled the island looking for a boat. Who the hell was after them?

WILLA FINISHED HER BATH although she was so exhausted that just drying off took all her effort. All the adrenaline rushes, being shot at, running for her life, being almost made love to—all of it was taking a toll on her body.

Her mind wouldn't shut down, though. Her thoughts circled around Landry refusing to rest. She'd been wrong about him. He'd saved her life twice now. How could she doubt him anymore?

She thought about Odell and what he'd said to her in his kitchen. He had been acting so strangely during the barbecue. Almost jealous. Maybe definitely jealous.

The truth was she had little to no experience with men. As much as she hated to admit it, Landry had been right about her. She'd dated some in high school, all neighboring ranch boys who attended the same church she did. A couple of them she would have let get to first base—if they had tried. They hadn't.

She'd heard a rumor her senior year that she was frigid. She hadn't really known what that meant since she felt anything but. The rumor had persisted, and by the time she went away to college, she'd started to believe it.

She seemed to intimidate men. At least some of them. Men like Odell, who seemed to put her on a pedestal and wanted to protect her. Not men like Landry Jones, she thought as she slipped on a cotton nightshirt and climbed between the covers.

Overhead she heard the creak of footsteps, but she didn't even give Cape Diablo's ghosts a second thought as sleep took her again, this time even more deeply than in the boat on the way back to the island.

LANDRY TOOK THE MAIN PATH down to the pier, then circled the island counterclockwise. He waded around fallen trees, mangroves, swampy bogs of quicksand and mud and finally rocks, sometimes having to almost swim to keep going.

As he reached the end of the island near the deep water cover, he spotted an older man. Carlos.

That was all he could remember. Carlos, the faithful friend, who had been given the right to stay on the island until he died—just like the old lady who lived on the third floor, Alma Garcia.

Willa said she'd seen the two talking, seeming to be arguing as if the old man was trying to convince the woman of something.

Now Landry watched Carlos pull his small fishing boat up on the beach. The elderly man seemed lost in his own world, making Landry wonder if both of the elderly on the island weren't senile. Or was that just what they both wanted everyone to think?

Did Carlos know the true story of the disappearance of his best friend, wife and children? Supposedly he and Alma hadn't been on the island when it had happened. Maybe that was true. Maybe Carlos was as much in the dark as Landry was about the events that had happened around him.

Landry stepped back into the trees as he watched Carlos look around then head into the thick underbrush. Where was he going?

Carlos wasn't gone but a few minutes before he returned with a fishing pole. He put it in the boat, then pushed out and climbed in.

The boat motor purred to life. Carlos spun the motor to point the bow of the boat toward a far island. He gave it full throttle and sped off to disappear into the horizon.

Landry waited for a few minutes longer, then trailed along the edge of the cove to the spot where he'd seen Carlos disappear into the underbrush. There was only a faint path, not even noticeable if you hadn't seen someone just emerge from it.

Bending low to avoid limbs, he pushed back through the dense vegetation. At first he didn't see it. Probably because the old fishing shack was grown over, the island reclaiming it.

He recalled how secretive the old man had been and felt a shiver of dread work its way through him as he reached for the door.

Chapter Thirteen

Landry found the latch on the old fishing shack and slowly opened the door.

The shack was small and dark inside. All he could see were old bait buckets, weather-ruined life preservers from another era, a few fishing poles and odds and ends.

He wasn't sure what he was looking for. Maybe an unfinished painting by W. St. Clair. One of him. Stolen from her room.

It was just large enough that he could step inside. He stood in the darkness, not sure what he was looking for, just that he didn't like this place any more than he did the villa.

The island gave him the creeps and he wasn't sure if it was the people on it—or the evil he felt that permeated the place. He hadn't been kidding when he told Willa he could feel that something horrible had happened here.

He found the small wooden box under a shelf hidden

behind the life preservers. The lock was rusty, the hinges creaking loudly as he lifted the lid.

Old letters. Envelopes yellowed with age. Gingerly he picked up one, lifted the flap and carefully pulled out the thin sheet of paper.

The letter was written in Spanish, but he could make out enough of it to see that it was a love letter addressed to "My Dear One" and signed "Your Faithful." The writing was neat but neither masculine or feminine, the paper plain.

He put it back in the envelope, noting that the letters had never been mailed. Had they been delivered?

Putting the letters back, he returned the box to its hiding place and checked to make sure no one was waiting for him outside. The island seemed too quiet, as if even the birds held their breath. It gave him a strange, anxious feeling, and suddenly he couldn't wait to get back to Willa.

Slipping out, he stole back out to the beach. No sign of Carlos.

After circling the entire island, he hadn't found any sign of another person on the island or a boat. Maybe there wasn't anyone on the island he had to fear. Not that he was taking any chances with the odd group living here.

For now they were safe here. Bull would be arriving soon with the package from the gallery owner. Once they had the painting it would just be a matter of getting the disk to the right people.

As he neared the villa, he felt the heat bearing down

on him. He needed a bath. The thought brought back an image of Willa in the tub. Not a good idea. A swim. That's what he needed. He would get Willa and go down to the sandy part of the beach. The tide was going out. It would be nice to swim and maybe lie in the shade for a while. Better than staying alone in that small apartment with her.

Henri's door was open, but there was no sign of her or of the others as Landry crossed the courtyard. Loud music throbbed from Blossom's apartment. There was no other sound as he climbed the stairs.

He tapped at the door, wondering if he would wake Willa. He'd been gone for quite a while. She should be awake by now. She'd been so obviously exhausted earlier he figured she'd gone right to bed.

"Yes?"

"It's me," he said quietly.

She opened the door, a paintbrush in her hand.

He stepped in, her look questioning. He shook his head. "You're working?" He glanced toward the bedroom and her easel, relieved to see a picturesque painting of the villa. No splashes of red. No hint of a bloodbath.

"Want to go for a swim?"

She cocked her head at him.

"We can talk on the beach." He made it sound as if he thought the apartment might be bugged. It might be, but that wasn't his reason for wanting out of here right now. Willa smelled and looked wonderful and the apartment was cool, the bed too inviting.

She studied him for a moment, then said, "I'll put on my suit."

When she came out of the bathroom, she was wearing a two-piece—chaste compared to that string thing that Henri was wearing yesterday.

But Willa in her two-piece was so damned sexy he felt poleaxed standing there looking at her. How the hell was he going to keep his hands off her?

"What?" Willa asked.

He shook his head, afraid to trust his voice.

She picked up a beach cover from behind the door and pulled it around her, leaving nothing exposed but a lot of leg.

He turned away, let out a long breath and couldn't wait to hit the water. He just hoped it would be cold enough, he thought as he followed her down a short path to a secluded stretch of beach, the sun golden over the top of the palms.

Running past her, he dove into the surf. As hot as he was, it felt icy, but as he surfaced and looked back at Willa, he realized the dip had done little to cool his desire for her.

What was wrong with him? He'd gone all these years without needing anyone. Hell, he hadn't seen his family in months. Talk about a loner.

So now he was going to let some South Dakota farm girl twist him all up inside? A virgin farm girl, he thought with a grin as he waded toward her.

He plopped down on the beach and squinted out at the Gulf. Out of the corner of his eye, he watched her drop her beach cover and walk slowly into the surf. He closed his eyes and lay back in the sand, concentrating on each breath the way he did when he was shooting a sniper rifle.

Over the sound of the surf, the breeze in the palms overhead and the cry of seagulls on the rocks nearby, he heard her return from the water and lay down on the sand next to him.

The sun beat down on his bare chest, legs and arms. He tried to concentrate on the rise and fall of his chest as he breathed slowly, carefully, too aware of her next to him.

Whose stupid idea had this been? A secluded beach in paradise? What had he been thinking? At the time he'd thought anything was better than staying another minute in that small apartment with her.

He flinched as a cool damp fingertip touched his shoulder. Eyes still closed, he felt her shadow fall over him only an instant before her lips brushed his.

He opened his eyes and looked into a whole lot of blue. He'd been able to read her from the first time he'd seen her. She was incapable of hiding her feelings. Even her thoughts. Just as she wasn't hiding any now.

He groaned and cupped the back of her head as he brought her mouth down to his again.

She tasted salty, her palm cool as she rested it on his chest. He parted her lips with his tongue and drew her down on him, her cool body on his sun-hot one as he kissed her deeply, aroused by her lush body clad in the still-wet old-fashioned two-piece swimsuit.

As he freed her of the two-piece suit, he rolled over so he was on top. Tossed the suit aside—top and bottom— Her eyes widened a little as he pressed his chest to hers. She felt so good.

He'd promised himself he wouldn't do this. She must have seen his moment of hesitation.

"Are you sure about this, St. Clair?"

"I need a man who doesn't own any sheep," she said on a breath.

He grinned down at her. Damn, she was sexy as hell in that innocent, naive South Dakota way of hers. "What you need, darlin', is a man who can promise you tomorrow. I'm not that man."

"Don't go gallant on me now," she said, and grinned up at him. "I want you to be my first. Set the bar for those other poor fools."

He didn't want to even think about another man making love to this woman. He dropped his mouth to hers, stunned by the sensation of just kissing her, and all the while telling himself that this wouldn't change anything between them.

WILLA HAD OFTEN dreamed of the first time a man would make love to her. Frustration and fear combined. But kissing Landry, she let herself enjoy the feel of him, the new sensations that sent shock waves through her body, tremors of exquisite pleasure. She'd challenged him and he'd taken it. No other man would ever be able to surpass this, she thought as he dropped his mouth to her breast and she felt his wonderfully talented tongue begin its journey over her body.

After that, she had no clear thoughts. He touched and licked and caressed and kissed, leaving trails of heat up and down her body. She gasped, sometimes out of shock at the places he went, the things he did, until she lost herself entirely in the building volcano he'd started inside her.

And just when she thought she couldn't take any more, he made her explode, showered every cell in her body with pleasure as she quaked in the aftermath.

Then he kissed her, held her and started all over again. This time as she clung to him, he entered her. She felt a sharp jab of pain, then slowly he took her higher and higher until she could no longer hold back, the two of them, their bodies locked in ecstasy on her swimsuit cover, the warm sand beneath.

He rolled to the side, taking her with him, pressing her face into the sweaty warmth of his chest. She breathed him in so she never forgot his scent, the feel of him, the sound of his voice next to her ear. She never wanted to forget.

"Are you all right?" he asked.

"Hmm," she said. "I just feel sorry for those other men. That will be a hard act to follow." She giggled and tried to remember a time she felt this wonderful. "Not even Christmas in South Dakota could top this."

He chuckled, a deep throaty sound, and pulled her closer. She sensed a sadness in him. Did he feel guilty for taking her virginity? She smiled at the thought, grateful to him, not that she would ever tell him that. But it made her wonder if Landry Jones wasn't as tough as he let on. She let herself drift in a cloud of contentment, forgetting for a while that anyone wanted her dead.

HE MUST HAVE dozed off. Landry woke with a start as cold water dropped on his chest, on his face. He reached for the gun he'd wrapped up in his T-shirt as he squinted up at the dark silhouette standing over him.

His T-shirt was empty.

He came all the way up into a sitting position, eyes focusing as he raised one hand to block out the sun and saw Willa standing over him holding his gun. His gun with the *silencer* on it.

He swore and met her gaze.

"*You,*" she gasped as if she couldn't catch her breath. She was soaking wet, obviously having gone swimming. He hadn't felt her leave his side and that, it turned out, was a huge mistake on his part. "You're the one who shot at me."

She pointed the gun at him, her finger on the trigger. "I wondered when you didn't seem overly concerned about a killer being on the island with us. It was because you're the one who took those shots at me!"

He groaned. "I did it because I needed to gain your trust quickly."

"My trust?" She spat the words at him. "You took shots at me to gain my trust? Did you make love to me for the same reason?"

"You know better than that."

"Do I?" Her hand holding the gun was trembling. "You could have killed me."

"I'm a better shot than that." He gave her a grin, hoping to lighten this moment.

Her eyes narrowed, the gun in her hand steadied as she pointed it at his heart.

He wiped the grin off his face. "Look, I'm sorry I lied to you. I didn't know you then." He lifted up, getting his feet under him and slowly rising. "I was desperate and you were just a means to an end. But somewhere along the way, that changed." He reached out to her, needing to get that gun away from her before she accidentally pulled the trigger. Or pulled it on purpose.

She stepped back, the gun still aimed at his heart.

In the distance, he heard the sound of a boat headed this way. Bull. He glanced toward the sun. It was high overhead, bathing the island with golden heat.

"That will be Bull with the paintings," he said.

She nodded, her eyes sparking with anger and pain. She handed him the gun, slapping it into his palm, her blue eyes cold and hard enough to chip ice. "Let's get this over with."

Finally something they could agree on. She didn't give him a chance to say anything else, which was good because there was nothing he *could* say. He was a bastard. He liked to believe that all men were on some level, but right now he had the feeling he was wrong about that, too.

He stuffed the gun into his shorts as he watched her walk away, mentally kicking himself. As she was swallowed up in the vegetation, he quickly picked up his T-shirt from the sand, shook it out and went after her as he pulled it on.

His skin felt raw with sensation, their lovemaking imprinted on his flesh—and embedded forever in his brain. Talk about raising the bar. He couldn't imagine being with another woman without thinking of Willa and this sunlit beach.

WILLA HEARD HIM behind her but didn't turn. She had every right to be angry with him. It didn't matter that he'd done what he had for supposedly a higher purpose—getting the disk and taking down the bad guys. Or that he'd been shot defending himself and was now being wrongly accused. Or that there were still people out there who wanted him dead—and her, as well, and that he'd taken those shots at her to protect her. Or that he *had* protected her, even saved her life last night by the canal.

The bottom line was that he'd lied to her. He'd deceived her.

It wasn't him she was so angry with and she knew it. Nor was it the fact that she'd made love with him, wanted him to be the first man and wasn't sorry one iota for it.

No, what had her furious with herself was that she'd made Landry Jones into some kind of hero in her mind. She'd needed a hero and she'd let herself believe he was one.

And that hadn't even been her worst mistake.

No, her worst mistake was… She slowed, tears burning her eyes. She felt his hand on her shoulder and didn't even have the energy to shrug it off. He came around in front of her, his gaze going straight to her tears. He looked like his heart would break, as if he could read the truth in her eyes.

Her worst mistake was falling in love with him.

She jerked away from him and wiped angrily at the tears as she bit her lower lip and gave herself a good mental talking-to.

"You want me to pick up the supply box?" he asked behind her, sounding uncomfortable, as if half-afraid to touch her and even more confused as to what to say.

"You do that," she said, lifting her chin into the air and stalking toward the villa. She could feel his gaze burning into her backside. He'd looked scared back there, as if he couldn't bear what he'd done to her—but she would bet if she glanced back, he'd be looking at her butt. Landry, everything else aside, was all male.

She cursed his black heart silently as she passed through the archway and ran up the stairs. She heard Odell come out of his apartment to go down and get the supplies he'd ordered, but she hurriedly unlocked her door and rushed in before he could call to her.

She went straight to the tub and stood under the spray, washing away the sand and the scent of Landry Jones. If only it was that easy to wash away the feelings. They had come on her so quickly. But spending time with a man under a dock under these kind of circumstances put feelings on fast-forward. At least that was her excuse.

It didn't help that he was so darned handsome. Or often pretty witty. And that grin—

She shut off the water and heard the door to the apartment open. She'd left it unlocked so he could come in when he returned from the dock. The painting was in the box. Evan had said it was. So there was no more looking for the disk. Soon, no reason to be together.

She heard Landry cutting into the box and reached for a towel. Within moments, Landry would have what he wanted, and if she knew him the way she thought she did, he would be gone.

She leaned against the wall and waited for the sound of the front door closing. Maybe he'd already left and she just hadn't heard the door close. He could be halfway to his boat right now.

The bathroom door opened. Her heart did a little leap inside her chest. At least he had come to say goodbye.

He drew back the shower curtain, seeming a little surprised to see her standing in the tub holding a towel to her. She met his gaze and felt another start.

"The disk isn't in the painting."

"What?" She plowed past him out of the shower and into the living room, still holding the towel in front of her, indifferent to her otherwise nudity.

The box was open, a half-dozen of her paintings standing up along the front of the couch. The one painting, the one that Simon Renton had supposedly hid the disk behind, was on the floor, the back ripped, revealing the space under the paper. It was empty.

She bent down and picked up the painting, seeing at once where the paper backing had been slit. The disk *had* been inside it.

She turned to stare at Landry. He looked like he'd been kicked in the gut as he lowered himself into one of the chairs just feet from her.

"Where is the disk?" she said stupidly.

He shrugged. "Maybe it fell out. Maybe Simon lied. Who knows?"

She felt chilled suddenly. Putting down the painting, she went into the bedroom, closed the door and dressed. The ramifications were just starting to hit her. Without the disk, Landry could never clear himself. Both of their lives would remain in danger.

Unless someone already had the disk and that was why she and Landry were almost killed last night. They had become too much of a liability.

As she came out, she found Landry sitting in the chair, his head in his hands. She desperately wanted to ask him what he was thinking of doing now. But she was afraid to hear his answer.

"Okay," she said, unwilling to give up, needing something to do, to say. "What if the disk did fall out?"

He looked up at her as if she had to be kidding, even thinking there was somewhere to go from here.

"Seriously, what if it did?" She went over to the box

and looked inside, although she was sure Landry had already done that. "Then it must have fallen out before it left my studio, so it would be…" She glanced toward the box the police had packed, knowing the disk wasn't in the bottom of it. Both she and Landry had gone through that box, as well.

A thought struck her. "Why didn't the police know about the disk?"

"What?"

"You said the police didn't know about the disk so they wouldn't have been looking for it," she pressed. "But if you and Simon were working undercover to get information out about organized crime—and who the dirty cop was—then why wouldn't the police be on the lookout for a disk?"

"Because the disk just kind of fell into our laps from one of Freddy D.'s disgruntled associates. The guy contacted me but Simon insisted he be the pick-up man because I was too visible in the organization. He hadn't been in long and was low on the totem pole."

"So neither you nor Simon had told your bosses that you had the disk?" she said.

He nodded. "We hadn't gotten a chance. Then after what went down… The cops had no way of knowing how you were really involved. They would just assume you were in the wrong place at the wrong time."

"So…" she said, glancing toward one of the boxes that the police had packed for her. "If one of them picked up the disk, they would just think it was mine. All this time, we've been looking for a painting. Not a disk."

Landry watched her with interest now.

She stepped over to her box of supplies and dug down to the box marked "Bookkeeping." She came back to the table and set it down, half-afraid to open it for fear she was only going to get both of their hopes up for nothing.

Slowly she lifted the lid. Under all the papers was a small disk box with the imprint of one of the more popular home business accounting systems. Inside were a half-dozen disks.

"You own a computer?" Landry asked.

"A laptop. I had it shipped back to South Dakota. My stepfather was going to do my taxes for me if this dragged out until April. But I forgot to send him the disks."

Landry watched her as she removed the disks from the box and sorted through them.

Her fingers froze. She swallowed around the lump in her throat. "This one isn't mine." She handed it to him as if it were made of glass.

He swore. "If we had a computer we could check to see if it is the right one."

"Odell has a laptop." She remembered seeing it under his desk and wondering at the time why he was doing the book on an old typewriter instead of the computer.

Landry looked from her to the disk and back again. "You think you could distract him long enough for me to make sure this is the disk?"

She went to the window and peered out. Odell had come back with the supplies he'd ordered. Through a crack in the blinds she could see him unloading some things.

"Go out now. I'll call him up to my apartment and try to give you as much time as possible," she said, meeting his gaze.

He eyed her. "You're not thinking of—"

"Of course not. I'll think of something."

He nodded, something passing between them that felt like trust. "I'll come up as soon as I know for sure."

She smiled. He seemed to think she would be needing his help to keep Odell off her. "Take this." She tossed him her camera. "It will give me an excuse for you being gone."

Landry caught the small digital camera and tucked it into his pocket, then reached into the duffel he had by the end of the couch. "Put this someplace where you can get to it if you need it."

"I'm touched by your concern," she said, actually meaning it as she took the gun he handed her.

He grinned. "I know I really know how to treat a girl." And he was out the door.

Willa put the gun in a drawer in the end table by the couch, then waited until Landry disappeared before she went down the stairs to Odell's apartment. The door was partially ajar. She could see him inside putting food in the fridge.

"We owe you steaks," she said from the doorway and then tapped on the door slightly. "Sorry to catch you in the middle of something." She couldn't help but glance toward the typewriter. There wasn't any paper in it. Out of the corner of her eye, she caught a glimpse of the laptop right where she'd seen it before.

"Come on in," Odell said, putting the rest of his food inside and closing the fridge door. "Can I offer you something to drink?"

"Thanks. Landry took off to try to photograph the sunset and…" She feared she was a horrible liar and Odell could see right through her.

"Do you need something?" he asked, coming right over to her.

"You're going to think I'm silly, but I started to rearrange the furniture and I found a hole behind the couch," she said. At least that much was true. "I'm afraid there might be something in it. Like rats. Or—" she shuddered for real "—a snake?"

He smiled. "Do you have a good flashlight?"

She shook her head and he quickly went to his desk, pulled out a drawer and took out a large flashlight.

"Let's go see what's in your wall," he said, sounding excited—and not the least bit afraid of snakes.

"You're sure you don't mind?"

Odell laughed. "Not at all. I'm honored actually—" he said as she led him across the courtyard and up the stairs "—that you would ask me."

She felt guilty at once. He'd been nothing but nice to her and now that she knew he hadn't taken potshots at her, she felt even worse. But there was still that snake someone had put in her tub… "You have been so nice to me. I really appreciate it." She opened her door, let him go in and entered behind him, leaving the door open.

He stopped in the middle of the room. "You've

been through a lot, it sounds like. I figured you might need a friend."

She smiled at him. "I do."

Silence stretched between them as they just stood looking at each other. For a moment Willa had the strangest feeling that she might need the gun she'd hidden. She took a step toward it.

Odell seemed to come out of a daze. "The hole behind your couch. Right." He turned and surveyed the couch. "Looks even worse than mine."

All Willa could think about was Landry. Was he in Odell's apartment? She'd noticed that Odell had closed his door, but hadn't locked it—just as she knew he wouldn't. Unless he was working, his door was usually open.

She helped Odell pull the couch away from the wall. While he went behind it to peer into the hole, she stayed on the other side near the end table and the gun.

Landry, she realized, hadn't even asked her if she could shoot a gun. She guessed he'd just assumed that since she was from South Dakota…

"This is quite the hole," Odell said. "Goes back in quite a ways. Don't see any indication there has been any kind of creature in here, though."

"What do you think made it?" she asked, getting on her knees on the cushions to peer over the back of the couch.

To her surprise she saw that Odell had a small pocket knife in his hand. She recalled the knife cut in the tape on her box of supplies from the dock. Odell. He'd opened the box. That's how he knew she was an artist.

Was that also how he knew she was from South Dakota? Something in her supply box gave her away?

Or had Odell known long before then? Was she the real reason he'd come to Cape Diablo? And Landry thought Odell's interest in her was romantic. Willa suspected he couldn't be more wrong.

Odell sat down, his back against the wall as he looked at her. "I'd say a person made the hole in your wall."

"Why?" She tried to hide her surprise at seeing the pocket knife that Odell had folded and put into his pocket again.

"I don't know if you've noticed but the old gal upstairs doesn't just sneak around a lot at night," Odell said. "She's looking for something."

Willa thought about her missing painting. "Like what?"

"I saw her digging around the villa, poking in the walls," he said. "It wouldn't be that unusual for a smuggler and pirate like Andres Santiago to have hidden all kinds of things in these walls—gold, coins, even jewels or I suppose currency."

Willa feigned interest. "Are we talking a lot of money?"

He laughed and leaned toward her conspiratorially. "There are those rumors that Andres hid a small fortune on this island before his disappearance. Seems he didn't trust banks. So it's not too surprising that there were also rumors after that about fortune hunters who came out to the island disappearing, as well."

"You don't think—?"

"That the old gal would kill to keep a treasure she felt

was rightly hers? You better believe it. Not to mention the Ancient Mariner from the boathouse. I think he's in love with Alma. And we all know what a man will do to protect the woman he loves."

"That is very true," Landry said as he leaned over the couch to smile at Odell. "Honey, there is a man behind our couch. I hope you can explain this."

Willa hadn't heard Landry come in and obviously neither had Odell. Odell looked both startled and embarrassed, quickly getting to his feet and dusting himself off as he retrieved his flashlight.

"I found a hole behind the couch when I started rearranging the living room and I was worried there might be something in there," she quickly explained with a grimace. "Something icky."

Landry shook his head and grinned at Odell. "Just like a woman. What is it that makes them want to rearrange the furniture all the time?"

Odell shook his head. "Nothing in the hole to worry about anyway," he said to Willa, and smiled. "Let me know if you need help again."

"I doubt that will be necessary," Landry said, his smile gone. He tossed Willa her camera. "Got that photo you wanted, darlin'."

Odell left, but not before stealing a glance at Willa.

"You made him think I was coming on to him," she whispered the minute the door was closed.

"If I hadn't acted jealous, he would have been suspicious and you have to admit, having him look into a hole behind the couch is suspect. Brilliant," Landry added quickly. "But later when he's over there by himself, he's going to wonder."

She stared at him, trying to gauge what he'd found out, pretty sure by his mood that she already knew. "Was it the disk?"

He nodded. "I didn't have time to read it—just confirm that it is the disk that got Simon killed. And Zeke."

She saw the pain in his eyes. "I'm sorry."

He shook his head. "Finally the truth will come out."

She let herself breathe a sigh of relief, then instantly felt a stab of acute disappointment. If he had been telling her the truth about the disk and it clearing him, then all of this would be behind them once he turned it over to the police. He could go back to his life. She could go back to hers. Isn't that what they both wanted?

She told him her theory about Odell.

Landry didn't seem that surprised. Or that worried.

"What happens now?" she asked.

He pulled the disk from his pocket and turned it slowly in his fingers. "We get off this island." He looked up at her, pocketed the disk and smiled. "I'll go get the boat. Pack what you have to take and I'll pick you up at the dock."

She nodded, feeling a wave of doubt. Landry was leaving with the disk. She had the strangest feeling that he wouldn't be back for her. That she wouldn't ever see him again.

"Hey," he said, lifting her chin with his finger. "You don't think I'll come back for you?"

Mind reader. She opened her mouth. Nothing came out.

Landry looked disappointed in her as he reached into his pocket and took out the disk. He opened the drawer where she'd put the gun and put the disk in the back, then held up his hands to show that he wasn't doing some disappearing act with it.

"Lock the door behind me. I'll be back for you," he said and taking the gun with the silencer on it left.

Chapter Fourteen

The sun glided slowly across the sky toward the Gulf as Landry left. Wind moaned in the tops of the palms and the air seemed heavier, as if a storm was coming in. A big tropical one from the feel of it. He moved quickly, the growing storm making him all the more anxious to get off this island.

It was dark in the trees, the trail deep in shadow as Landry left through the archway, taking the path where he'd first found Willa.

So much had changed since then. *He* had changed. He couldn't believe she'd found the disk. Even if the painting would have made Willa's show, the disk wouldn't have been in it. Landry shook his head, imagining how that would have gone over if he'd purchased the painting and found no disk inside.

Now all he had to do was get the disk to the right people. No small chore since someone knew where they were. Those shots at them in Everglades City had been to kill. They couldn't go back there.

As he reached the beach where he'd hidden the boat, he realized what had been nagging at him all day. Why hadn't the shooter followed them to the island to finish the job?

He froze as he looked into the bushes and saw that his boat was gone and knew why the shooter hadn't followed them to the island.

Because there was already someone planted on the island to make sure he never left here with the disk.

His mind racing, he ran toward the old fisherman's shack. As far as he knew Carlos's was the only other boat on the island. He had to get Willa and the disk off this island and fast and he hadn't heard Carlos return to the boathouse. Landry would check this side of the island before heading back. With luck he would find the old man and persuade him to either take them off the island—or lend them his boat.

Who was the killer on the island? Odell? The guy would be his first choice. Willa wouldn't let him back in the apartment again, would she? What about the women? Either of the women looked like they could bite a man's head off in a single bite.

As he reached the beach where he'd seen Carlos pull up his boat, Landry saw that it was empty. No boat. No Carlos.

He'd been so sure he would find the old man here, get the boat and get back to Willa. Once they were on the water, he planned to head up the coast. He'd rather take his chances out in the Gulf than go back to Everglades City.

But now he worried that there was no way off the island. No boat. No chance to get the disk into the right hands before it was too late.

Landry swore and started to turn back toward the trail and the villa when he saw something in the water. His pulse jumped as he stepped toward it. A piece of dark fabric washed in the waves. Kneeling down, he reached into the water and grabbed a piece of the fabric, half-afraid it would have a body attached to it.

He lifted out the black top Blossom had been wearing and looked toward the storm-blackened horizon for her body, his heart in his throat.

Dropping the top back into the water, he dove through the trees for the villa. He didn't know what the hell was going on but he had a bad feeling the killer on the island was about to make himself known.

Landry hadn't gone but a few feet when he heard a noise off to his right. He wasn't alone.

Hoping a moving target would be harder for whoever was out there to hit, he took off in a crouched run down the winding trail.

WILLA COULDN'T SIT still. All she wanted to do was get off the island with the disk. She could come back for anything she left behind.

She dressed for the boat ride, packed a few essentials, then waited for Landry, listening for the sound of a boat and growing more anxious every minute when she didn't hear one.

It was the quiet that eventually got to her. Blossom wasn't playing her music. In fact, Willa had seen neither Blossom nor Henri all day.

She peeked out through the blinds. A light was on at Odell's apartment. She could see it through his partially opened doorway. But no sign of him, either. The villa was too quiet.

Her heart began to pound. Where was Henri? And Blossom? And why didn't Landry come back?

Her fear growing, she went to the end table and took out the gun he'd left with her. She checked to make sure it was loaded, thankful that Landry had been right. She did know how to use a gun.

Darkness settled over the villa. She realized there was someone else she hadn't seen—or heard all day. Alma Garcia. There was no light that she could see on the third floor. Where was everyone?

She glanced again at Odell's. No sign of life. He must have gone somewhere with Henri and Blossom, though she couldn't imagine a more unlikely trio. As she waited, she fought the need to find one of them just to reassure herself that everything was fine.

Wait until Landry comes back.

She went back to the couch and had just sat down when she heard the scream. Leaping up, she ran to the window and looked out. She could see Henri down by Odell's open doorway. Henri was walking backward, her hands over her mouth, a wounded animal sound coming out of her.

Grabbing the gun and keeping it by her side out of

view, Willa opened the door and stepped out on the balcony.

"What is it?" she called down to Henri.

The redhead spun around, terror in her eyes. Her hands fell away from her mouth and she began to cry as she stumbled to the bottom of the stairs, sitting down on the bottom step. "It's Odell," she managed to say between sobs. "I think he's dead."

"Did you check for a pulse?" Willa called down.

Henri looked up at her, her face pale, her eyes red from crying and shook her head. "I couldn't. I faint at the sight of blood and there's blood all over." She started crying again.

"I thought you left. I haven't seen you all day," Willa said as she descended the stairs behind the other woman.

"I had a hangover," she said, sniffing and wiping her face on the sleeve of her robe. "I took a sleeping pill with some wine. It knocked me out."

"Have you seen Blossom?" Willa asked.

Henri noticed the gun and shook her head slowly. "She was with Bull earlier. But I thought Bull left alone."

"Okay," Willa said, and with the gun still at her side started across the courtyard toward Odell's open doorway. She listened for the sound of a boat, praying that Landry would return before she reached Odell's apartment.

She saw no one, heard no boat motor. And Landry should have been back by now.

Willa glanced back. Henri now stood in her apartment doorway looking scared.

"Stay there," Willa said unnecessarily to Henri as she neared Odell's open doorway. "Odell?" she called. "Odell?"

At the door she stopped, took a breath and let it out slowly, her fingers tightening on the grip of the gun. With her free hand, she pushed the door open with one finger. It swung in.

The smell of blood hit her first.

The second thing was Odell lying on the floor, his typewriter next to his head. Henri was right. There was blood everywhere.

Willa stepped in trying to ignore the blood as she hurried to check Odell's wrist for a pulse. She could see that the side of his head had been smashed in and there was blood on the typewriter and the sheet of paper was sticking out of it. Like Henri, she fainted at the sight of blood under normal circumstances.

She had just touched his wrist and found what she'd expected—no pulse—when the typed words came into focus. She drew her hand back as she read the byline: Odell Grady, *St. Petersburg Times* Investigative Reporter.

Below it was the beginning of a newspaper story about her and Landry. No wonder Odell Grady had to have a paper every day. A news junkie, huh?

A sound startled her. She couldn't tell where it had come from. But it had sounded like hurried movement. Her gaze flicked to the cool shadows at the back of the apartment. The killer wouldn't be foolish enough to hide in here. After Henri had found Odell and come for help, the killer would have had plenty of time to get out. Unless, of course, he was waiting for Willa.

She heard the sound again, so close it made the hair stand up on the back of her neck. She swung around as a hand dropped to her shoulder. She screamed, her hand tightening on the gun, her finger going to the trigger.

"Easy, darlin', it's me," Landry said as he caught the gun before she could turn and fire.

He looked past her to where Odell Grady was sprawled on the floor, clearly dead. "Was it something he said?"

She buried her face in Landry's chest. He put his arms around her, holding her tight.

"I didn't hear the boat."

"My boat is gone and the old fisherman hasn't returned."

She drew back to stare in shock and fear at him.

"Not to worry. We're getting out of here," he said as he drew her out of Odell's apartment and into the courtyard. "Where are Henri and Blossom?"

"Henri's the one who found Odell. She's in her apartment. No one has seen Blossom since she was talking to Bull earlier." Willa seemed to choke on a sob. "Odell lied. He was a newspaper reporter. He was doing a story on us."

Landry heard the panic rising in her voice. "Okay," he said, sounding much calmer than he felt. "Let's go get Henri and see if we can find Blossom."

She nodded as he pocketed her gun and they started across the courtyard toward Henri's apartment.

"Her door's closed," Willa said, slowing. "When I left her it was open. She was standing in the doorway, waiting for me."

Landry felt his pulse jump.

"She said she fainted at the sight of blood."

He wondered why Willa hadn't. Because she could be strong when she had to be. He was counting on that.

There was no light coming from inside Henri's apartment and the storm had snuffed out the sun, filling the courtyard with a kind of ominous darkness.

Landry tapped at Henri's door, realizing he couldn't hear the power generator. The only light in any of the apartments was one on the third floor. An old oil lamp, he thought, watching the light flicker.

Someone had shut down the generator. Or forgot to refill it with gas. Either way, it didn't bode well, given that Odell Grady had been murdered and it appeared Henri was now missing. He didn't even want to think about what had happened to Blossom.

He tapped again. No answer.

"She wouldn't have left, Landry," Willa cried, grabbing his arm. "She was upset and scared and she said she would wait."

Right. Unless she killed Odell and Blossom.

He tried the knob. It was unlocked. Pushing open the door, he took the flashlight from his pocket and shone it into the room. "Henri?"

No answer but then he hadn't expected one.

The apartment was smaller than Willa's, the bathroom door standing open, the shower curtain pulled back exposing an empty shall. Henri was gone.

"Let's try Blossom's." He knew she wasn't going to answer the door but he could hope.

He knocked, then tried the knob. Also unlocked. He was starting to see a pattern here. He pushed open the door and shone the flashlight in. The light bobbed around the small apartment with the same results. Empty.

"Okay," he said seeing the fear in Willa's eyes. "Where is the disk?"

"In my pocket. I thought it would be safer on me."

He smiled down at her. "Good." As he glanced toward the third floor, he couldn't help but recall the noise he'd heard out in the woods. Someone had followed him back here.

Through the third-floor window he saw a shape cross in front of the lantern light. "I think we'd better pay a visit to the old gal upstairs," he said, and handed her back the gun he'd taken from her earlier. "Just in case."

WILLA DIDN'T LIKE the stormy darkness that had settled over the villa. Or the fact that Landry had given her a weapon. She could see her own fears mirrored in his face as the wind whipped the tops of the palms in a low howl.

Landry thought Henri and Blossom were dead. She had seen it in his expression when he'd checked their apartments.

She glanced up the stairs. It was the last place she wanted to go. But she also knew that Landry wasn't about to leave her alone while he checked on the old woman. Look what had happened when she'd left Henri alone.

Willa had seen someone upstairs—just a dark shape silhouetted against the lantern light for an instant. The old woman? Was it possible Henri had gone up there? Maybe Blossom, too.

As she started up the stairs, Willa couldn't shake the feeling that going up there was a mistake. Someone could be waiting for them. What if it was the old woman? With all that digging for treasure, Alma could be stronger than any of them suspected. Strong enough to lift an ancient manual typewriter and kill Odell.

At Alma's door, Landry tapped softly. No answer. He tapped again. Willa thought she could hear music playing faintly inside the apartment.

Landry tried the knob. The door swung open and Willa was hit with an old musty smell. But what surprised her were the furnishings. It was as if time had stopped in this room thirty years ago.

"Alma?" Landry called. No answer. Willa felt her stomach clench as she and Landry moved through the living room deeper into the apartment toward the sound of the music. Alma must be in the area over Willa's apartment. She could see a closed door at the end of the room. The music seemed to be coming from behind there.

"Wait," Landry whispered.

She had reached for the knob on the closed door, but when she turned she saw that Landry had stopped in front of a painting on the wall.

Her *unfinished painting!* The one stolen from her apartment.

Landry was frowning at the painting, no doubt rocketed back to the night he killed his partner, Zeke Hartung.

Willa closed her hand over the knob to the closed door just before she heard the rustle of fabric off to her right and swung her head in the direction of the archway into the kitchen.

Alma Garcia came flying out of the kitchen, a butcher knife clutched in her fist, her eyes wide and wild.

Willa had just enough time to jump to the side as the woman rushed her. She caught a glimpse of Landry's surprise as the woman spun on her heel, more agile than Willa would have expected, given her apparent age.

Alma lunged for Willa again, but Willa managed to get one of the living room chairs between her and the knife-wielding woman. She could see that the older woman's hands were shaking, the knife blade flickering in the light from the oil lamp.

Landry grabbed Alma from behind. He said something to Alma in Spanish. The knife fell to the floor and he kicked it toward Willa who quickly picked it up, her heart in her throat.

The older woman's eyes filled with tears. She shook her head and answered him in English. "I will never leave you. Kill me so that my spirit might remain here always."

Landry spoke again in Spanish, cajoling. Alma began to cry. He let go of the older woman.

"Come on. We'll have to leave her," he said. "Henri and Blossom aren't here."

Willa moved to the door, keeping an eye on the woman and vice versa. She put the knife down as she went out the door, the scent of another time wafting out as Landry closed the door.

They went back down to Willa's apartment. Landry checked to make sure they were alone before he locked the door.

"You don't think Alma killed…"

He shook his head.

She saw something in his expression and felt her stomach lurch. "What aren't you telling me?"

"I found that crocheted black top of Blossom's floating in the water by the old fisherman's shack."

Willa covered her mouth with her hand. "Henri?"

"At this point, I'd say there's a good chance she's our killer."

Willa shivered. Outside her window, the wind howled, the palm trees slapping the side of the house, the air inside the apartment seeming too thick to breathe. They were on an island, trapped with a killer. "What do we do now?" she asked in a whisper.

He cocked his head and went to the window, opening it. The wind blew in, making the blinds flap. "That sounds like the old fisherman's boat motor."

"I don't hear anything," she said, trying to listen over the wind.

"Carlos didn't come in at the boathouse. The wind

is carrying the sound from the cove. With the storm getting worse, he would be smart enough not to try to get back around the island by boat."

Fear jolted through her. "But that's exactly what you're planning to do. Let me go with you."

He shook his head, grinning. "Me and boats are like that," he said, crossing his fingers and holding them in front of her. "Not to worry, I'll be back before you know it."

She looked at Landry, suddenly even more afraid because she knew what he was thinking. "Henri will be waiting for us knowing, we're trying to get off the island. That's why you won't let me go with you."

He brushed cool fingers over her cheek, his gaze locked with hers. "I want you to stay here. Lock the door. And if anyone, and I mean *anyone* tries to get in, shoot them." He released her hands to pick up the gun from where she'd set it down, and he pressed it into her palm.

"Landry—"

He cut her words off with a kiss. Pulling back he gave her a grin. "I'll be back. I can't bear the thought of all those other men competing with me if I don't."

She couldn't help but smile. She leaned into him, aching for him. Right now she just wanted him to hold her and never let her go but she was smart enough to know their only chance was to get off the island. Everyone was dead except a killer, a crazy old woman and a possibly equally demented old fisherman. Neither would be of any help.

She and Landry were on their own against— That was just it. They had no idea what they were up against.

Landry let go of her and moved to the door. He checked out the window first. The sky was dark with the storm. She could hear the roar of the Gulf as he opened the door. Past him, darkness pooled in the corners of the courtyard.

Henri could be out there anywhere.

Landry glanced back at her. What she saw in his eyes tore at her heart. But before she could say a word, he was out the door, locking it behind him.

She stood in the middle of the room feeling bereft, listening for…what? Gunfire? That pop she'd become so familiar with? A grunt? A cry?

She could hear nothing over the wind as it rattled the windows and rain began to pelt the glass. Overhead she heard the squeak of floorboards and froze.

LANDRY MOVED through the rain and stormy darkness, quiet as a cat. If he didn't make it back to the villa he feared Willa wouldn't stand a chance. Whoever had killed the others would wait her out. The supply boat wasn't scheduled to come back for days. There would be no one on the island who could help her because unless Landry missed his guess, the old fisherman and his boat would disappear, as well.

The wind groaned in the trees overhead, the canopy swaying above him. He could hear the rain hitting the leaves, but couldn't feel it except through the occasional hole in the canopy. It was dark under the storm and trees, the air thick and humid, buzzing with mosquitoes.

He tried to see ahead, to listen for the sound of a killer stalking him. He could hear nothing but the storm and see nothing in the darkness that lay ahead.

Moving swiftly, he ran along the trail, his gun drawn. He was surprised when he reached the cove and saw that the boat was pulled up on the beach. No sign of Carlos.

Landry made a run through the driving rain to the boat, he pushed it out, jumped in and started the motor.

Carlos appeared out of the dense vegetation. He seemed confused. He didn't go for a gun. Nor did anyone else appear. No bullets whizzed past as Landry turned the boat out into the huge waves that now swelled in the cove. It would be a rough trip around to the pier. An even rougher trip up the coast once he had Willa.

And the disk.

For a while, he'd almost forgotten about it.

Rain soaked him, the driving wind chilled him. He hit a large wave and spray cascaded over him, salty and cold. He rounded the end of the island and looked back.

He could see no one as he pointed the boat toward the first channel marker. Getting the boat had almost seemed too easy. So why hadn't Henri tried to stop him? His fear spiked at the obvious answer.

Because Henri had her sights set on someone else.

The person who had the disk. Willa.

Chapter Fifteen

The floor overhead groaned. Willa could hear someone moving around on the floor above her. She stared upward, her heart pounding.

Something was different. When Alma had been up there moving around, the floor hadn't groaned like this.

Willa stumbled over to the table where she'd put down the gun. She picked it up, holding it in front of her as she stared at the ceiling.

Someone was up there. Not the old woman. Someone heavier. The floor groaned. She could hear the footfalls reverse their path across the floor and then there was silence.

Willa jumped as something crashed into the door behind her. She heard a cry then the faint words, "Help me."

Her heart leapt to her throat as she moved to the door. "Who's there?"

"Help me."

She reached for the doorknob, remembering Landry's admonition not to open the door no matter what.

Hurrying to the window, she looked out. Blossom lay at her door. She was soaked to the skin, wearing nothing but a black bra and black jeans, barefoot, holding her hand to her side, bleeding. The gun bumped against the window.

Blossom looked up at her, pleading in her gaze as she mouthed, "Help me."

Willa looked past Blossom at the storm-whipped courtyard, the rain sheeting down, and made the only decision she could. She put down the gun and hurriedly opened the door.

Blossom hadn't moved, her eyes closed and for one horrible moment, Willa thought the girl was dead.

"Blossom!" She knelt at the girl's side, glancing at the balcony, afraid Henri would appear out of the rain.

Blossom's eyes fluttered. Willa grabbed Blossom by the feet and pulled her into the apartment, slamming the door and locking it behind them.

"Henri," Blossom said, her voice faint.

Willa knelt again beside the girl. "How badly are you hurt?"

"Stabbed," she whispered, and Willa saw that Blossom had both of her hands clutching her side.

"I'll get the first-aid kit." Willa ran into the bathroom and found the kit where Landry had used it. It was a small metal six-inch square can her mother had sent with her when she'd left home. Her mother had personally stocked it with items she feared her daughter might someday need.

As she turned, she heard a sound as if Blossom had bumped into the kitchen table. The table where Willa had left the gun.

On impulse, she slipped the disk from her pocket and hid it in the bathroom in a small hole behind the toilet.

Then she turned and stepped out of the bathroom, the first-aid kit in her hands.

Blossom stood at the table, the gun in her hands. A red stain ran down her bare skin where the stab wound should have been.

Willa looked from the woman's white unmarked skin to the gun pointing at her and finally met Blossom's gaze.

It was the first time she'd seen those eyes without the black coils of hair covering most of her face.

She was older than she had appeared before and the hand holding the gun was strong and sure.

"Where is Henri?" Willa asked, fear making her throat tight and dry. She was still holding the first-aid kit.

Blossom didn't seem to notice. Nor did she seem to hear Willa's question. She appeared to be listening, as if she heard—

Willa froze as she picked up the sound of a boat motor. Landry! He was headed for the dock.

"What do you want?"

Blossom focused on her and smiled. "Don't screw with me. I want the disk."

Willa looked down at the first-aid kit in her hands. She could hear the boat motor growing louder. She couldn't let Landry walk into a trap. Nor could she give up the disk.

"So all of that stuff about you being a star was just bunk?" she asked as she stepped a little closer to Blossom.

Goth Girl smiled. "Gotta admit I am one hell of an actress."

"You work for Freddy Delgado?"

Blossom laughed. "Yeah, right."

Willa was close enough that she could have gone for the gun. If she'd been crazy. "Well, you're not a cop."

"Not hardly. Come on, let's get this over with before your *boyfriend* gets back," Blossom said, still pointing the gun at Willa's heart.

"I guess you won't be needing this," Willa said looking down at the metal first-aid kit in her hands. She'd popped the lid, remembering the small sharp metal objects her mother had put in the kit: scissors, clippers, tweezers, pins. Everything a South Dakota girl might need in the big city.

Blossom's gaze went to the first-aid kit just an instant before Willa flung it at her face. Willa had expected to hear the boom of the gun as she slammed into Blossom, driving her back. Taken by surprise, Blossom fell over the chair behind her and went down hard. The gun skittered across the floor and disappeared under the couch.

Willa launched herself at the door, grabbing the knob and jerking the door open. She caught only a glimpse of Blossom scrambling to her feet with a knife in her hand as the door slammed behind her.

LANDRY BROUGHT THE BOAT into the dock, fighting the waves kicked up by the storm. The wind howled as rain lashed down. He could barely make out the villa through the driving rain as he hurriedly secured the boat to the lee side of the dock and ran up the beach.

His mind had been racing ever since he'd taken the boat and started back. So much about the missing disk and the people after it hadn't made any sense. But as he'd fought the storm waves, running the boat back as fast as he could without swamping it, he'd had time to think.

His thoughts had taken a turn that had curdled his stomach. He had to be wrong.

He heard a creaking sound off to his right and swung his weapon as he turned toward it, half expecting Henri to come at him out of the storm.

He couldn't make out what it was but he slowed, moving toward the sound. *Creak. Creak. Creak.*

And then he saw it.

His heart leapt to his throat and he let out a cry of alarm as the body swung into view. Henri. She hung by her neck from a rope tied to the ornate wrought iron along the front of the villa. Her body swung in the wind.

Henri was dead?

If Henri hadn't killed Odell and Blossom, then…

THE STEPS WERE WET and slick. Willa fell, tumbling down the last few. She scraped her arm on the wrought-iron railing and cut her leg open. Her blood mixed with the rain as she struggled to get to her feet. Behind her, she heard her apartment door bang open. In a flash of lightning, she saw Blossom silhouetted against the storm. The light caught on the knife blade, glittering wickedly as Blossom descended the stairs at a run.

Willa was on her feet but Blossom leapt over the stair railing, tackling her and taking them both to the tile next to the pool. Willa rolled Blossom over, both hands on Blossom's wrist holding the knife as she tried to wrestle it away from her.

But Blossom was strong and had obviously done this before. She bucked Willa off, throwing them both over the lip of the pool and into the putrid water.

Willa gasped as she hit the surface, dragged under by Blossom as they continued to fight for the knife. She opened her eyes but could see nothing in the darkness at the bottom of the pool as she and Blossom struggled.

Something brushed past her arm, wet and slimy. She choked, desperately needing air, but unable to let go of Blossom and the knife. She felt dizzy and could feel her grip weakening. And suddenly she saw something next to her in the water. The waterlogged face of the little boy from the photograph.

LANDRY SPRINTED through the arch into the villa, fear propelling him like a rocket into the courtyard.

Through the pouring rain, he glimpsed the two forms struggling by the pool, heard the splash as the two fell in.

Blossom and Willa.

He ran and dove headfirst into the rain-dimpled dark water. It was pitch-black beneath the surface. He swam blindly toward the spot where he'd seen the two go under, shoving away limbs and leaves that had decayed in the pool, feeling as if he was swimming through a decomposing soup.

His hand brushed against something that felt like hair and he brought himself up short as he felt pain slice across his arm.

Blossom had a knife and appeared to be frantically trying to swim to the surface, but something was holding her down. He didn't see Willa anywhere.

Hurriedly he swam around Blossom, staying out of reach of the knife she was swinging in a frenzied arch.

No Willa.

He could barely make out Blossom, who was fighting desperately to free herself from something he couldn't see. Needing air, he surfaced, and in a rush of relief, saw Willa hanging on the edge of the pool, choking and gasping, but alive.

He swam to her, pulled her into his arms. "Are you hurt?"

She shook her head, blinking through the driving rain at him as he let her go and pushing himself out of the water, pulled her out beside him.

He took one last look into the pool as he helped Willa up the stairs. The water had stilled except for the rain falling on it. Just below the surface he could see the dim gleam of silver from the knife still clutched in Blossom's hand and her hair floating around her pale face.

Landry turned away from the look of horror on her face and helped Willa into her apartment.

"You're bleeding again," she said, her voice sounding far away as she slumped into a chair.

"I'm fine." He locked the door and stooped to pick up the contents of the first-aid kit. His arm wasn't cut badly but he knew he had to get some disinfectant on it after being in that pool. "Come on."

He helped Willa to her feet and undressed her and himself on the way to the bathroom. Turning on the shower, he regulated the water then climbed in with her. They stood, holding each other as the water washed over them. Slowly he began to soap her wonderful body, desire washing away the horror of what he'd seen in the pool, the terror of what could have happened if Willa hadn't fought off Blossom and somehow escaped to the surface. How had she done that? he wondered.

Something in the pool had saved her.

He shook off the thought as she took the soap from him and began to lather it over him. He closed his eyes.

LATER, LYING IN BED, warm and dry and sated, his arm bandaged, his heart beginning to slow, he looked over at Willa. Her blue eyes were filled with tears.

Alarmed, he sat up and stared down at her. "What is it? Did I hurt you?"

She shook her head, her lips turning up a little at the corners as she looked at him. "You could never hurt me."

He wasn't so sure about that.

"So much death," she whispered. "I have seen so much death."

He pulled her into his arms and held her tightly. "The storm is letting up. We have to leave here. The disk? I know you had it in your pocket. It wasn't there when I undressed you. It must be in the bottom of the pool, huh?"

"I hid it in the bathroom."

He let out a breath, not realizing how afraid he'd been that the disk had been lost, that all of this had been for nothing. "Then everything is going to be all right." He drew back to look at her. "We survived it, darlin'."

Willa looked into his dark eyes and cupped his cheek with her palm. Her heart felt as if it would break, she loved him so much. She'd been afraid in the pool. Not for her own life, but Landry's. Willa had known she couldn't fight Blossom off any longer in the pool. She was out of air, weak and losing hope.

"What is it?" Landry asked.

She wanted to tell him about what she'd seen in the pool. About what had happened when the boy had appeared. But she couldn't bring herself to say the words.

"Can we please get off this island?" she said instead.

He smiled and nodded. "The rain sounds like it is letting up. We should be able to see well enough to make it up the coast."

She started to pull away from him, but he drew her close again and kissed her.

"I'll get the disk," she said. Everything else could stay here. She could buy new art supplies. If she ever painted again.

THE RAIN HAD STOPPED by the time they were dressed and ready to leave. Landry got the gun from under the couch, insisting she keep it on her. "Just in case."

She tried to tell him she wouldn't be able to pull the trigger even if she had to. Not today. But she'd taken the gun and stuffed it into the pocket of her jacket.

Landry led the way out of the apartment. Willa glanced down at the pool and quickly looked away. She felt a chill as she followed Landry down the stairs, and when she looked up she wasn't surprised to see the face at the window on the third floor.

Alma Garcia looked terrified, her eyes appearing even more crazed in the glow of the lamplight. She was staring at the pool as if hypnotized. Willa shuddered as she realized that the elderly woman had seen everything. Even the child in the water who had drowned thirty years ago?

Willa grabbed Landry's arm as they hurried from the courtyard. The boat was at the dock. She could see a strip of green in the distance as the other islands appeared from out of the storm.

"Don't get in yet," Landry said as he began to bail the water out of the boat.

She stood, afraid to turn around and look back at the villa for fear of what she might see. Landry was bent over, scooping rainwater from the bottom of the boat. She could tell by his movements that he wanted off this island as badly as she did.

The dock swayed. Willa froze as she realized that

someone had just stepped onto it. No. She squeezed her eyes shut, shoving her hands deep into the pockets of her jacket. *No.* This was going to be over as soon as they reached the mainland. It *had* to be over. She felt powerless, too close to the edge. She couldn't take any more today.

She opened her eyes as the dock swayed again. Landry was still bent over, unaware they were no longer alone.

Slowly she turned and gasped as she recognized the ghost moving down the dock toward her. It was the man who'd come into her art studio that night before her gallery showing.

"Hello," Simon Renton said.

Landry swung around, his hand going for his gun.

"I wouldn't do that if I were you," Simon said.

Landry froze, his face a mask of shock and then slow realization. "No."

Simon laughed. "Sorry to disappoint you. I'll take that disk now."

"Why?" Landry asked on a breath, not moving to give him the disk.

"Isn't it obvious? I'm *dead* and that disk is worth a small fortune on the market."

"You'd sell it to Freddy D.'s competitors?"

"Or Freddy D. if he can come up with enough money."

Neither man seemed to have remembered Willa was even there. She could understand why. She felt small and insignificant, huddled in her jacket, standing on the end of the dock next to the boat watching the two as if all of this was nothing but a very bad nightmare. Any minute she would wake up and be in her art studio apartment upstairs planning her showing that coming night.

"You were the dirty cop," Landry said with a shake of his head. "Not Zeke. But why did he try to kill me?"

"Could have been because of the information I leaked to him about you. I told him not to trust you. That I'd heard you were shopping the disk and that if you got your hands on it...." Simon shrugged.

"Zeke tried to kill me."

Simon nodded. "I thought he just might. He hated dirty cops." He held out his hand. "I'll take the disk now."

"Without the disk, I will always be a hunted man," Landry said.

"But you'll be alive."

"Will I?" Landry said with a laugh. "You can't let me live. You know I'll go to the cops, the feds, I'll tell them about you faking your death. How did you do that anyway?"

"It's all about money. You pay the right guys the right amount and they will find a homeless guy your size, even get him a tattoo just like yours," Simon said with a grin as he lifted his shirt, exposing a dragon tattoo that curled around his side. "All you need is two not real bright goons to help you fake your death and tell their boss they killed you."

"T and Worm. So why didn't you go back and get the painting and the disk that night then?"

Simon sighed. "It took a while to convince them they

would be better off playing on my team. By then it was morning and I needed to lay low. After all, I was dead. But I knew if I sent the info to Freddy D. he'd send you to get the disk. And if I could depend on anyone to get it, it would be you." He wiggled the fingers of his outstretched hand. "Come on, Landry. The disk for your life and your girlfriend's here."

"You're the one who hired Blossom—or whatever her name was."

Simon smiled. "What happened to her anyway? I really thought I'd be hearing from her and not have to take things into my own hands, so to speak. Doesn't matter. You can give me the disk or I can take it off your body. Which is it going to be?"

The gunshot startled Willa, bringing her out of her lethargy as she saw the bullet punch the water's surface next to the boat.

"Landry!" she cried, afraid he'd been hit.

"It's okay, darlin'," he said, not looking at her. "You want the disk, Simon. Fine. But let her go. I'll start the boat. You let her get in and leave. Then I will give you the disk."

Simon smiled. "So it's like that, is it?"

Landry reached back and pulled the cord on the motor. The air filled with the throb of the engine. Holding up his hands, Landry stepped from the boat and reached for Willa's hand, his gaze meeting hers.

She saw the warning, felt it in his body as he drew her to him, wrapping his arms around her tightly for a moment before helping her into the boat. She stood in the boat, numb from the cold, the terror, the exhaustion.

"You can drive a boat, can't you? Keep land in sight until you reach a town," he said. "Keep going." He shoved the boat out.

She swayed and almost fell as the boat drifted slowly away from the dock. She steadied herself as she saw Landry reach in his pocket for the disk. *No.*

She reached into her pocket for the gun.

It was gone.

Landry. He'd taken it. He'd known she would try to kill Simon. And probably fail.

She was floating away, the motor on the boat idling. Did Landry really believe that Simon would let him go? Let her go, as well? Simon would come after her. She and Landry knew he was alive. He couldn't let either of them live.

Landry started to hand Simon the disk.

She grabbed the handle on the motor, spinning it around as she'd seen Gator do, and hit the throttle. The bow of the boat shot up. She couldn't see the pier but she heard a startled sound come from it as the boat roared toward the two men.

The bow hit the pier and sent a shockwave through her as it glanced off throwing her to the side. As she fell she heard the pop of a gun going off. It was the last thing she remembered before waking up in Landry's arms.

Epilogue

Landry walked out of the police station, stopping on the steps to breathe in the warm Florida morning. He was free. Free of false charges. Free of being an undercover cop.

He wasn't sure how he felt yet. Everything that had happened had taken its toll on him. He wasn't sure he would ever get over Zeke's death. Or Simon's for that matter. Landry had ended up killing them both. They'd been his partners. He'd trusted them.

It had taken days to make his statement. Thank God for the disk that proved that Simon was the cop who'd gone bad—not Landry. Not Zeke. It was little consolation. A lot of people had died unnecessarily, Zeke among them.

The body of Blossom—real name Angela Warren—was brought up from the bottom of the pool on Cape Diablo. The police found that part of the baggy black garb she'd been wearing as her Blossom disguise had gotten caught on a large limb that had fallen into the pool.

Landry remembered the look on Willa's face when she'd been told that. She didn't seem to believe it. He wasn't sure he did when he recalled how Blossom had been fighting to surface, striking out at water as if she thought someone was holding her down.

Blossom, that is Angela Warren, turned out to be a young prostitute whom Simon had once arrested. A hundred thousand dollars was found in her checking account supporting what Landry said about Simon hiring Angela to pose as Blossom at Cape Diablo to get the disk—and get rid of Willa and Landry.

Odell, it was assumed, had either run across Angela as an investigative reporter and recognized her when she came to the island or let it slip what he was working on and it had gotten him killed.

Henri had been exactly who she said she was. Nothing more than a guest on the island. While Landry had been suspicious when she'd pretended to be drunker than she was, he suspected she was just hoping Odell would take advantage.

Maybe she really had come to the island thinking she wanted solitude to get over her recent breakup. But once she'd met Odell she must have decided she wouldn't mind a little male comfort. Instead, she'd only met death.

Henri had definitely picked the wrong island for any kind of peace. Willa had made the same mistake. Only, he thanked God, with a different ending.

While Willa gave her statement and was released,

Landry had been held for more questioning. With the information on the disk, the police and feds were able to throw a wide net over organized crime in Florida, bringing down Freddy D. and his associates and underlings, except for T and Worm.

Their bodies were found in a dump, both shot, gangland-style, in the back of their heads. Freddy D. no doubt had heard about Simon Renton's "second" death on Cape Diablo and realized T and Worm had double-crossed him.

When the cops were finally satisfied with what was on the disk and Landry's and Willa's statement, the chief broke the story, dragged him in front of the blazing lights of the media and gave him a medal. The story made headlines across the state. He was a hero.

He hadn't wanted any of it.

But once labeled as a dirty cop, it took a hell of a lot of fanfare to clear his name and he wanted that more than anything. He *needed* that before he could go find Willa St. Clair.

He'd heard she'd gone back to South Dakota, some tiny town he couldn't even find on a map. He'd had to fly into the capital of Pierre at the center of the state and rent a car, driving north until he spotted a grain elevator with Alkali Butte printed on it.

After that, he'd only had to ask for directions, then taken a series of dirt roads until he spotted the white farmhouse on the horizon and slowed to pull into the drive.

WILLA HEARD THE VEHICLE pull into the farm yard and looked up from her painting to see the unfamiliar car stop in a cloud of dust.

She'd never thought she'd come back to South Dakota. But after everything that had happened, she realized a true home didn't have to be one you'd been raised in all your life. It was anywhere there were people who loved you.

Her mother and stepfather had been wonderful through all of this. She'd seen how much her stepfather loved her mother and it had made her realize she'd never given him a chance.

Being around family had helped her regain her strength if not heal her aching heart. But she was painting again and that she knew was a sign that she would be all right.

"Who's that?" her mother called from the kitchen. The house smelled of homemade bread and beef stew since it was almost suppertime.

"Someone lost," Willa called back as she put down her paintbrush. No other unfamiliar cars ended up in the yard otherwise. "I'll take care of it."

She left the small room off the living room where she'd set up her studio and walked to the door, pushing open the screen to squint out at the car, the sun glinting off the windshield.

The driver's door slowly opened.

She blinked, her heart soaring as Landry Jones climbed out. Over the weeks since she'd seen him she'd heard he'd cleared his name. But she'd never expected to see him again. Because she never planned to go back to Florida. And she'd never dreamed he'd come all the way to South Dakota.

"Hello, darlin'," he said, stopping on the bottom porch step. "You're a hard woman to find, Willa St. Clair."

She tried to swallow the lump in her throat as tears welled in her eyes. "Landry, what—" That's all she got out before he was up the steps and she was in his arms.

"I love you, Willa St. Clair," he said, and then he was kissing her.

Behind her she heard the screen door creak open. "This must be Landry Jones," she heard her mother say. "I'll set another plate." The screen door closed with another creak.

Landry pulled back from the kiss and grinned at her. "I already like your mother," he whispered. "But then I adore her daughter."

Her heart leaped.

Landry turned serious. "I quit my job. I've got some money saved, though. But at this moment, I have no plans for the future." He grinned again. "Except one."

Willa held her breath and thought about the painting on her easel inside the house. She hadn't painted since she left Cape Diablo. Until this morning.

On her easel now was a painting of a two-story white house, a tire swing in the big tree next to it, an assortment of toys scattered across the green lawn. There were red-and-white gingham curtains at the kitchen window and a man and woman sitting together on the front porch swing. They were faceless, the painting not yet finished.

"Willa," Landry said, and swallowed.

She'd never seen him nervous before.

"I know the timing is awful. Why would you want to marry a former undercover cop, let alone one who is jobless and isn't even sure what he's going to do now?"

"Landry," she said, smiling up into his wonderfully handsome face. "Is there something you wanted to ask me?"

He laughed. "Oh, yeah, darlin'. Would you consider being my wife? I love you. I need you. I don't care what tomorrow brings as long as I'm with you." He dropped to one knee. "Marry me, Willa St. Clair."

She laughed as she cupped his face in her hands and leaned down to kiss that amazing mouth.

"Was that a yes?" he asked as she pulled back from the kiss.

"No," she said as she drew him to his feet, wrapped her arms around his neck and started to kiss him again. "*This,* my love, is a yes."

* * * * *

Look for the exciting conclusion to
the CAPE DIABLO *trilogy, next month*
in Joanna Wayne's A CLANDESTINE AFFAIR.

Experience the anticipation, the thrill of the chase
and the sheer rush of falling in love!
Turn the page for a sneak preview
of a new book from Harlequin Romance
THE REBEL PRINCE
by Raye Morgan
On sale August 29th
wherever books are sold.

"OH, NO!"

The reaction slipped out before Emma Valentine could stop it, for there stood the very man she most wanted to avoid seeing again.

He didn't look any happier to see her.

"Well, come on, get on board," he said gruffly. "I won't bite." One eyebrow rose. "Though I might nibble a little," he added, mostly to amuse himself.

But she wasn't paying any attention to what he was saying. She was staring at him, taking in the royal blue uniform he was wearing, with gold braid and glistening badges decorating the sleeves, epaulettes and an upright collar. Ribbons and medals covered the breast of the short, fitted jacket. A gold-encrusted sabre hung at his side. And suddenly it was clear to her who this man really was.

She gulped wordlessly. Reaching out, he took her elbow and pulled her aboard. The doors slid closed. And finally she found her tongue.

"You...you're the prince."

He nodded, barely glancing at her. "Yes. Of course."

She raised a hand and covered her mouth for a moment. "I should have known."

"Of course you should have. I don't know why you didn't." He punched the ground-floor button to get the elevator moving again, then turned to look down at her. "A relatively bright five-year-old child would have tumbled to the truth right away."

Her shock faded as her indignation at his tone asserted itself. He might be the prince, but he was still just as annoying as he had been earlier that day.

"A relatively bright five-year-old child without a bump on the head from a badly thrown water polo ball, maybe," she said defensively. She wasn't feeling woozy any longer and she wasn't about to let him bully her, no matter how royal he was. "I was unconscious half the time."

"And just clueless the other half, I guess," he said, looking bemused.

The arrogance of the man was really galling.

"I suppose you think your 'royalness' is so obvious it sort of shimmers around you for all to see?" she challenged. "Or better yet, oozes from your pores like...like sweat on a hot day?"

"Something like that," he acknowledged calmly. "Most people tumble to it pretty quickly. In fact, it's hard to hide even when I want to avoid dealing with it."

"Poor baby," she said, still resenting his manner. "I guess that works better with injured people who are half asleep." Looking at him, she felt a strange emotion she couldn't identify. It was as though she wanted to prove something to him, but she wasn't sure what. "And anyway, you know you did your best to fool me," she added.

His brows knit together as though he really didn't know what she was talking about. "I didn't do a thing."

"You told me your name was Monty."

"It is." He shrugged. "I have a lot of names. Some of them are too rude to be spoken to my face, I'm sure." He glanced at her sideways, his hand on the hilt of his sabre. "Perhaps you're contemplating one of those right now."

You bet I am.

That was what she would like to say. But it suddenly occurred to her that she was supposed to be working for this man. If she wanted to keep the job of coronation chef, maybe she'd better keep her opinions to herself. So she clamped her mouth shut, took a deep breath and looked away, trying hard to calm down.

The elevator ground to a halt and the doors slid open laboriously. She moved to step forward, hoping to make her escape, but his hand shot out again and caught her elbow.

"Wait a minute. *You're* a woman," he said, as though that thought had just presented itself to him.

"That's a rare ability for insight you have there, Your Highness," she snapped before she could stop herself. And then she winced. She was going to have to do better than that if she was going to keep this relationship on an even keel.

But he was ignoring her dig. Nodding, he stared at her with a speculative gleam in his golden eyes. "I've been looking for a woman, but you'll do."

She blanched, stiffening. "I'll do for what?"

He made a head gesture in a direction she knew was opposite of where she was going and his grip tightened on her elbow.

"Come with me," he said abruptly, making it an order.

She dug in her heels, thinking fast. She didn't much like orders. "Wait! I can't. I have to get to the kitchen."

"Not yet. I need you."

"You what?" Her breathless gasp of surprise was soft, but she knew he'd heard it.

"I need you," he said firmly. "Oh, don't look so shocked. I'm not planning to throw you into the hay and have my way with you. I need you for something a bit more mundane than that."

She felt color rushing into her cheeks and she silently begged it to stop. Here she was, formless and stodgy in her chef's whites. No makeup, no stiletto heels. Hardly the picture of the femmes fatales he was undoubtedly used to. The likelihood that he would have any carnal interest in her was remote at best. To have him think she was hysterically defending her virtue was humiliating.

"Well, what if I don't want to go with you?" she said in hopes of deflecting his attention from her blush.

"Too bad."

"What?"

Amusement sparkled in his eyes. He was certainly

enjoying this. And that only made her more determined to resist him.

"I'm the prince, remember? And we're in the castle. My orders take precedence. It's that old pesky divine rights thing."

Her jaw jutted out. Despite her embarrassment, she couldn't let that pass.

"Over my free will? Never!"

Exasperation filled his face.

"Hey, call out the historians. Someone will write a book about you and your courageous principles." His eyes glittered sardonically. "But in the meantime, Emma Valentine, you're coming with me."